The Secrets of Earth House

THE ELEMENTALISTS • BOOK 2

MICHELLE JARVIS

Love all, trust a few, do wrong to none.

— WILLIAM SHAKESPEARE, *ALL'S WELL THAT ENDS WELL*

Contents

One

Rosalinde had never been a good student. She was clever, sure, and she could retain information if she wanted to. But that was the problem. She'd never *wanted* to until now. As she made her way through the darkened halls lit only by dancing torchlight, she cursed her foolishness yet again for not throwing herself into learning when she was younger as much as she had devoted herself to extracurricular activities.

The library door was unguarded at this time of night. To be honest, she wasn't sure if they guarded it at any time. Who would want to steal books? Except her, of course, because that was what she was there to do.

It wasn't that she wanted to steal from her own library, but Rosalinde didn't have a choice. There were too many unanswered questions swirling about, too many things she didn't know, and no one to ask. Ros didn't know who she could trust; therefore, stealing the information she needed seemed like her only option.

Ros slipped into the dark room and felt her way down the wall until she reached the first of the stacks. She let her hand drop to her side and counted the books that her fingertips grazed. At the thirteenth book, she stopped and kneeled on the floor, pulling books thirteen, fourteen, and fifteen out of their places. Reaching farther back into the shelves, Ros withdrew the small lantern she'd hidden there earlier in the week.

She focused her attention on the tip of her finger, willing it to burn. To her delight, a tiny flame appeared and lit the lamp. Her brief time with the Night mages had revealed that she had access to more gifts than just the Tsunami power she'd been trained to use since childhood. She was excited to try the new gifts, but wasn't sure how to home in on the skills required for each element.

Training as a Water house mage left her completely lacking in the basics the other houses taught their Elementalists. After all, what good was learning to use a magic you couldn't wield? She would make do with the library as her teacher now.

Finding books about elemental training was the straightforward part of her quest; in fact, she'd already read the basics on Air, Fire, and Earth. But there was little to find about the Night house and the secrets it held, no matter where she looked. There also wasn't much to find on the other things she was researching—Cradles, the powerful places where the elemental powers were strongest, or Moonchildren, like the creature Ros had met in the woods after the vuljasari attack.

Rosalinde looked down at her palm, her eyes tracing the scar upon it. The circular shape Whimsy had left as a reminder coincided with the phases of the moon. Tonight, it was waning gibbous, leaving her only the last quarter of the month to figure out a wish to have the fae creature grant.

She'd considered asking for her father to be returned, just as she had initially thought to use the wish, but she wasn't sure what sort of danger she'd be bringing him into. Her father might not be home, but he was safe wherever Larkin Zolto was keeping him. Of that, she was sure. Larkin had proven herself a false friend after these many years, but even after all that happened, Ros knew she wouldn't hurt King Tancred. She might be a liar scheming for the throne, but Larkin wasn't a killer. At least, Ros didn't think so, though her instincts regarding Larkin had been woefully lacking thus far.

For now, Ros believed her father was safer away from the castle, even if it meant putting her last grain of faith in Larkin Zolto.

The other wish that had filled her heart and mind these last few weeks was to see the Night mage. She had planned to choose him as the winner of the Great Match, until the Earth house had blackmailed her, but he didn't know any of that. All he had seen was Ros naming another man to be her husband. If she used her wish to ask the fae for Cassian, even just to speak to him one more time, what might she say? Apologizing seemed like the best place to start, but saying she was sorry was pointless when she was betrothed to someone else. Though she was truly sorry, saying it wouldn't change the outcome of what had happened.

She wanted to ask about his mother, Ombretta, and Gaius, the strange darkness with ties to both of them. Her mind had endlessly played through the possibilities of what might have happened in the forest afterCassian removed her from it, and none of the scenarios were good.

But she couldn't ask. She couldn't waste her wish on something so selfish, no matter how desperately she wanted to.

Instead, she returned the books she'd hidden under her skirts and searched the library for new information about the fae children and their gifts, looking for a way to make the best of the boon she was given. Most of what she'd found were children's stories or elaborately detailed encounters that felt miles from her own experience. She took them anyway, stuffing them into the bag she'd fashioned under her robe and nightgown. There were too many eyes around the castle, too many people with questionable allegiances, and she had some secrets that needed keeping.

As she snuffed out the lamp and returned it to its

hiding place, she felt a tingle run up her spine. She spun on her heel, water instinctively springing to her fingertips. Ros couldn't see anything in the darkness and she cursed under her breath at her folly. She'd been so careful in getting to the library, but once she was swept up in its contents, she hadn't paid close enough attention to her surroundings.

Gathering her nerve and leveling her voice, Ros asked, "Who's there?"

The room was quiet in response. Overwhelmingly so. The stillness was stifling, too heavy all of a sudden, and Ros felt the silence pressing in all around her. Her pulse raged in her ears as she strained to hear whatever or whoever was there.

"Cassian?" she whispered, hope igniting in her chest for one brief moment, only to extinguish the next. She knew he wasn't there, no matter how much she wished for him. No, if a member of Night house *was* there, it wasn't him.

"Gaius?" she asked, swallowing hard as a lump formed in her throat. She had no desire to fight him again, especially without knowing what had become of the rest of Night house while in the Cradle.

But Gaius didn't answer back. No one did.

As her eyes adjusted to the darkness, she couldn't make anyone out. She moved to the door and slipped through, tiptoed back through the hall to her bedroom, and locked herself inside. Even after lighting every lamp in the room and spreading them around so there were no pockets of shadow in the whole place, Ros couldn't shake the feeling that someone was watching her, and that she was woefully unprepared for whatever would happen next.

It had been two weeks since they had crowned her the Queen of Talabrih. Two weeks her father was still missing, two weeks with her deceitful future husband and former best friend at her side, two weeks without a glimpse or whisper of Cassian's fate or what had happened in the woods. She'd been locked up in the castle, her only moments to herself spent in the library, and now those were tainted after what happened the night before. The worst part was that she couldn't be entirely sure she hadn't imagined the whole thing.

Once she was named queen, she'd expected to have a free hand over decisions within the kingdom, or at least over matters in her own castle, even if she was being blackmailed. Instead, Ros had found herself under tighter reins than ever before. When she could escape the counselors and nobles vying for a position closer to the throne, she still had a retinue of guards at her back. After having one ruler kidnapped out from under their watch, they were hesitant to let her go more than a few feet without someone tagging along. It didn't help that at every turn she was bombarded with those who sought her favor, who begged her decision on matters her father had deftly avoided, or those who requested an audience with her for dozens of reasons both great and small.

Before she'd found the safety and relative privacy of the library, she'd tried sneaking off to the garden. Unfortunately, that seemed to be the haunt of promiscuous nobles and several times she'd had to sneak behind a hedge to avoid witnessing more than an innocent eyeful. She was nearly positive she'd seen her sister, Elsabet, sneaking around once or twice, but the glimpses were too quick to be certain and she did not know who Elsa's paramour might be. She knew her sister was old enough to make those sorts of decisions for herself, but knowing it and seeing it were two very different things. The very idea of her sister sneaking around with a lover made Ros uneasy, so she was glad she'd never seen enough to confirm anyone's identities.

The kitchens were a no-go as well. There always seemed to be a servant or guard making their way to or from there these days. Ros wondered if her mother had designed it that way after catching Ros sneaking off to find her father a few weeks ago.

That venture had been a disaster. Those helping her on her journey had been hurt, their lives endangered by a living darkness that had seemingly joined with Earth house to remove her father from the throne and secure their Elementalist as Rosalinde's royal husband. She still wasn't sure what the connection was and how everything fit together, but at this point, it didn't matter. Her nightly trips to the library could give her information on how to move forward, but not how to change the past.

Rosalinde pushed away her blankets and the dark thoughts hovering over her. So much had happened in such a short time, and she had trouble focusing on one bad thing without another rearing its head. Still, she had things to do; her revenge wasn't going to plot itself.

As Rosalinde made her way to the hall for breakfast after getting little to no sleep, she noticed that everywhere she looked this morning she saw Earth Elementalists. There had always been a few around the castle to work with her mother or act as ambassadors between the houses, but now it seemed that more than half of the castle's inhabitants were from her future husband's house. It was unnerving, especially after her excursion last night in the library and the feeling of being watched. Maybe it hadn't been a mysterious Night house entity, but simply an Earth house spy. At this point, they all felt equally evil.

She looked down at her palm and the drop of her father's blood that Cassian had somehow activated. It still pointed the direction it always had—toward the Earth house castle. When she'd been out searching for King Tancred, it hadn't registered in her mind that the blood would truly take her to the Earth house. She'd expected some secret hideout along the way, a forgotten stronghold with bandits or villains or mythical creatures holding him captive. If only she could go back in time to before things had fallen apart and tell herself where it was leading her.

Truthfully, she wasn't sure her old self would have believed it, even if someone had warned her. Larkin's betrayal was something she never would have predicted if she hadn't seen it with her own eyes.

Now she knew anyone was capable of betraying her. Maybe they already had. The Queen Mother was surprisingly quiet about the missing king now that Ros was betrothed to an Earth house mage. It was common knowledge that Queen Mother Sariyah had wanted her daughter to marry from the house she'd grown up in. Another Earth house royal would cement their connection to the throne, gaining them honor and wealth as the other houses courted favor through their royal son. Sariyah had never hidden her desire to give support to Earth house, but could she have really been part of the plan to abscond with her husband?

Then there was Elsabet. Rosalinde's younger sister disappeared daily on secret missions, and Ros did not know where she was going or what she was up to. Whatever information she was obtaining, who was she reporting to? Ros had noticed her spending a surprising amount of time with Larkin over the last few days, which was unusual considering how much they normally argued and seemed to dislike one another. It left Ros putting a wall between herself and Elsa, afraid of the younger girl's intent. They had never been close, but Ros had never believed her sister would seek to harm her or sabotage her happiness. Now she wasn't so sure.

It wasn't as if Elsa was knocking down Rosalinde's door to talk to her or prove her loyalty. Aside from the compulsory dinner each day with the nobles who still lingered from the Great Match, and the glimpses she'd caught of Elsa sneaking around the gardens, Ros couldn't remember their last interaction. But her sister had saved her from a quick marriage to Zandor by proposing they get married at the impromptu Great Match the kingdom would hold in a few months, and that rescue from fate's awful hand had to mean something. If she was actively plotting against her, on her mother's behalf or someone else's, a speedy union would be beneficial. Ros reminded herself of that every day, trying to find a pinprick of hope that *someone* was on her side, amidst the gloom that was now so pervasive around her.

If her sister was true, Ros would be okay. She only needed one person to believe in.

"Good morning, my love," Zandor said.

He stood in front of the doors leading into the great hall, a wide smile upon his chiseled face. He wore dark pants and a tan tunic that glinted with gold embroidery as the light caught it. It was finely made, probably by the palace's tailor, and the color stood out beautifully against his dark skin.

Ros hated herself for noticing how handsome he was, especially knowing what a horrible person hid inside the pleasant-looking outside. She had no confirmation he was in on the plan to kidnap her father and put himself on the throne at her side, but if her former best friend of over ten years was willing to betray her for the chance at power, the likelihood that he wasn't part of the plan was incredibly slim. Part of her wanted to just come right out and ask him, but no matter what he said, she wouldn't believe him either way.

She forced a smile onto her face and said, "Good morning, Lyzandor."

His smile wilted, faster than a blink, but it returned with vigor as he asked, "Feeling well today, darling? You look as if you didn't sleep well."

She pressed her lips together, holding back the curses she longed to throw at him. Ros knew her face gave away her feelings. She didn't have the ability to hide her thoughts like her mother and sister. So, even as she straightened her face in an attempt to hide her hatred for this man, she knew at least some of it was still exposed.

"It has been difficult to sleep, considering my father is still missing. My thoughts are rarely on anything else."

She watched his face for any indication of guilt, but the jerk actually managed to look concerned. The nerve of him! Ros turned and entered the hall, Zandor trailing behind her.

"If there's anything I can do..." he began.

"No," Ros said, cutting him off. "Your family has done enough."

She didn't bother looking at him this time, didn't

need to see the guilt that he clearly didn't feel. Instead, she sat down and started on her breakfast in silence, letting her rage stew as the rest of the Zolto family joined Zandor at the other end of the table.

Let them enjoy their breakfast, relish their time in the court's favor; soon enough, Ros would have her father back. She didn't know how, and she didn't know when, but she knew that as soon as she did, justice would find the Zolto family and her retribution would be swift.

Two

Despite her coldness toward her betrothed, Zandor invited Rosalinde to go for a walk in the gardens after breakfast. She wanted to make up an excuse, or better yet, flat-out refuse, but she couldn't. She needed to be seen with her future husband, to put in some time with him in front of the nobles. Her absence could lead to doubts in the other houses about the validity of her betrothal, and ultimately, the validity of her succession to the throne. She needed to play the role assigned to her, be the right sort of person to ascend to the throne, even if it meant dealing with outdated traditions that had no real impact on her ability to be a good leader.

Rosalinde knew that Air house was looking for a reason to turn on her. Hessian Barclay, the Air house ruler, had been nipping at her father's heels for years. Without her father there to keep him at bay, Ros wasn't sure what Barclay might do. She couldn't risk showing any weaknesses whatsoever, and a rift between Water and Earth houses was definitely that.

As they stepped into the garden, Zandor held out his arm for Ros to take. Despite the bile rising in her throat, she took his proffered arm, and they strolled out into the mid-morning sunlight. The gardens were lively today, vibrant and colorful, with new blossoms likely added by the influx of Earth house mages. Though the blooms were lovely, they paled compared to the wild and beautiful garden at Ombretta's home.

The thought of the Night house ruler sent a pang through Rosalinde. She barely knew the woman, but the memory of her out in the woods fighting her own child haunted Ros. Without knowing what happened after Cassian whisked her to safety, Ros was left to wonder about the fate of all the Night house members.

"Your mind is elsewhere," Zandor said, leaning toward her ear.

Ros jolted at his words and his closeness. "Sorry," she said, though she wasn't in the slightest. Any thought that took her away from him and this current moment at his side was appreciated, even if they were painful.

"Don't be sorry," Zandor said. "I can't imagine what you're going through right now. If my father was missing, I'd be beside myself with worry. I'm amazed you're holding up so well."

She dropped her arm from his and turned to face him. Ros wanted to set him on fire where he stood. If she had better control over all the elements, there's a chance she would have. It was bad enough that he was complicit in the scheme to kidnap the king and use his absence to gain a position of power, but to then pretend he sympathized with her situation was reprehensible.

Ros opened her mouth to give him the verbal lashing of a lifetime. He might be willing to do these things for the throne, but that didn't mean she had to let him off easy. If Zandor wanted to play the part of the villain, she would remind him every day of his evil deeds.

"Hello, brother."

Larkin's voice cut through the words Ros was ready to say. Rosalinde's former best friend's greeting wriggled into Rosalinde's brain, reminding her of every time they'd walked these gardens together, gossiping arm-in-arm as they avoided whatever they were supposed to be doing. Ros didn't bother looking up; she had no desire to see the girl who had betrayed her trust.

"Larkin, what a lovely surprise," Zandor said. "Even more surprising to see you, Lord le Fevre." Rosalinde's gaze *did* shoot up when Zandor said, "Florian, I thought you left with the rest of Fire house."

She took in the two standing before her. Larkin's hair was loose and natural, wild and full and beautiful; it was a change from her usual braids, and Ros couldn't recall the last time she'd worn her hair this way. She wore a lacy summer dress that left little to the imagination. Her figure was exquisite, and draped across Florian as she was, Ros would've assumed they were lovers if Florian didn't appear so uncomfortable. He dripped his customary charm, so perhaps the others had not noticed the rigidity of his shoulders and the forced way his lips were curled up. But after her time with him outside the castle, she could see the cracks in his mask now. Something was definitely wrong.

"I did, but then we received word that Ambassador Voclain had taken ill and we needed to send a replacement."

"Couldn't the Healers take care of him?" Ros asked, concerned. Voclain had been the Fire house ambassador for as long as she could remember. He was in the castle so often, he was practically an uncle to her.

Florian shrugged, giving Ros a half smile, but no further answer.

She pursed her lips. "And the Fire house's first son was sent in his place?"

His smile turned mischievous as he said, "It was suggested that we might have a strong kinship after our experiences together."

The meaning behind his words wasn't lost on Ros. Her father had a "strong kinship" with Florian's great-uncle, who had his own apartments in the castle near to the king's rooms. And though her mother's "strong kinships" changed through the years, her most recent was an Earth house mage of middling power who'd been frequenting her mother's chambers on and off for the last year.

Florian was meant to be her bed-mate.

Ros was certain the Zoltos would pick up on the insinuation as well, and she was terrified they would turn their ire on Florian next. Though she'd spent little time with him prior to their trek into the wilderness, she'd learned a great deal about who the Fire house noble truly was when he was out from under his father's thumb, and she would be devastated if harm came to him.

"It will be a pleasure working with you to form a mutually beneficial relationship between our houses," Ros said, hoping to deter any further conversation about any other kinds of associations.

"Yes, My Queen," Florian said, taking Rosalinde's hand and bowing to kiss it.

She felt rough parchment slip into her fingers as he pulled away. Ros curled it into her palm and moved her hand behind her back to tuck the note under the edge of the belt on her dress. She was itching to take it out and look at it, knowing it offered a reprieve from her boring day. But Florian had made a point of being secretive, so she would wait until she was by herself, despite her curiosity. Whatever was written on that paper was meant for her alone.

"Would you like to join us for the rest of our stroll?" Zandor asked, smiling at his sister.

Ros looked at Larkin, whose caramel eyes were directed right at her. She knew the look, the questioning nature of it. They'd spent years perfecting the ability to talk to one another without a word. Ros clenched her jaw in response, answering the unspoken question. It didn't matter how much had happened between the two girls, Ros would not let Larkin worm her way back into her good graces, not with little expressions, grand gestures, or anything in between.

Larkin gave a small nod, understanding and resignation clear on her face. "Thank you, but I think it's best for you and Queen Rosalinde to have time to yourselves."

"Come on, Lark," Zandor said, grabbing her elbow. "Why are you suddenly so formal? I didn't think I'd be able to pry you away from her side after she chose me, but instead, you've hardly been around."

Ros furrowed her brows in confusion. Zandor talked as if he didn't know why there was a rift between them, but how could that be?

Her eyes met Larkin's again, and in a secret, silent way, Larkin laid herself bare. Ros read her face, shocked at the truths she uncovered: Zandor didn't know about her father, about the blackmail. He was innocent of the whole thing. She'd been punishing him for the crimes of his sister. Surely, she wasn't working alone. If so, why wouldn't she have come to Ros before the Match and told her what was going on? Ros would've trusted her plan and sided with her without question.

It made little sense, unless someone else was pulling all the strings. But if Zandor wasn't involved with the plan to take power, who was, and what did it have to do with Larkin?

"There's a lot going on behind the scenes. More than

you know. I've been busy trying to get it all taken care of," Larkin said to Zandor, though Ros was sure the words were really for her.

"What could be more important than spending time with your brother and your best friend?" Zandor asked.

Larkin swallowed hard and forced a smile. "The good of the kingdom is in all our hands, brother, and I must do my part. Everything I do, I do for Talabrih."

Three

They said their goodbyes to Larkin and Florian before taking another turn around the garden. Ros did her best to be more courteous to Zandor, but she was too distracted to offer much of herself. Her head was swimming with the new information about the Zolto siblings. Though Larkin had implied her brother was innocent of everything, and that she was working for some greater good, could she really believe those things after all that had happened?

When she finally made it back to her room, she tore open the curtains and lit all the lamps, banishing any sign of shadow. Cassian had spied on her once, and after last night's uneasy feeling of being watched, she wasn't taking chances that someone else may have a similar ability of which she was unaware.

With the room as bright as the garden had been, Ros reached under her belt and pulled out the note Florian had passed her. She unfolded the parchment and her eyes pored over the handful of words in a rush. He wanted to meet her in the stables at midnight.

Ros chewed on the inside of her cheek, unsure what to make of Florian's message. Maybe he had received word from Cassian, or knew something about her father. Maybe there was a different reason they had sent him back as ambassador. Or maybe he was doing his duty to make arrangements to become her consort. If that was the case, did she really want to meet him in the middle of the night and encourage that course of action?

Florian was an attractive man, with thick blond hair and golden eyes that sparked with the Fire of his element. He was lithe, despite the sturdy chest and broad shoulders, and Ros couldn't deny that having him as a bedmate wouldn't be a *terrible* thing. But since Cassian had told her he wanted to be with her and only her, that he wanted to be devoted to their love, she couldn't stand the thought of being with anyone else.

It hadn't always been that way. She'd grown up knowing that even after she was wed, she'd have the opportunity to find pleasure in the arms of other nobles. Monogamy wasn't expected within the noble houses unless it was a love match or an agreement had been reached. Marriages were often built to forge relationships with the other houses, not trying to find love for the individuals involved. It wasn't something people talked about in the open, but it was *known*. Ros had always been okay with that resolution until she met the Night mage.

Now she wanted no one else.

Ros read the note again. She already knew she would meet Florian in the stables. Whatever he had to say, it would still be more excitement than she'd had in weeks, even if she ended the night by slugging him. With Florian le Fevre involved, it was definitely a possibility.

THE REST of the day moved so slowly that Ros thought it must be some magical curse disrupting the flow of time. She moved through the sluggish hours with a prickly energy bouncing inside her, eager for the opportunity for something *different*.

When darkness fell and the castle's inhabitants finally retreated to their slumber, Ros dressed herself in a tight-fitting jumpsuit like the ones used in the Great Match. She hoped the attire would give her cover against the night, as well as provide anonymity if someone saw her sneaking into the stables. It was bad enough for the princess to be sneaking out to meet a man in the middle of the night, but the queen should be more dignified than that—her chosen lovers should come to *her*, not the other way around—even if it was for something entirely different.

She made her way down the hall from the royal quarters and slipped into the servants' stairway rather than taking the grand staircase. That was a surefire way to get caught. Instead, she slinked down the steps and hoped she wouldn't run into anyone doing late-night chores.

The servants in the castle were well-compensated for their work and had been for hundreds of years, since the first Water house king took the throne and declared that Elementalists and magicless alike should be paid fairly for their work. Rosalinde's mother had given steady wage increases through her years as queen, which meant most of the servants were loyal to her and would report Rosalinde if they saw her out at night. Though Ros was now the queen and should be able to do as she wished, the Queen Mother was holding onto small vestiges of power however she could.

Ros wasn't sure how nervous she should be about that. The transition to the throne had been easy, her mother passing the crown without fuss. Looking at it now, even after only a couple of weeks, it seemed almost too easy, as if the process had been nothing more than ceremonial. Yes, she was constantly bombarded with issues, but they were mostly small, petty things that others could decide if she knew who to trust. It made her wonder who was making the big decisions, and if they had been doing so for far longer than the time her father had been missing.

But that was a problem for a different day. Right now, she needed to get out of the castle and into the stables without getting caught.

She stepped off the staircase by the great hall and headed for the exit. She was nearly there when she saw torchlight approaching from outside, dancing on the stone walls ahead of her. Ros jumped back against the wall, feeling her way down the shadowed hall as the light grew ever closer. She needed to turn and run. She knew it, but she couldn't make her body listen to her brain. She was afraid of echoing footsteps, the certainty of getting caught. If she could just get back to the stairs...

A massive hand clamped over her mouth at the same time another grabbed her arm. She tried to pull away from her assailant, but they were too strong. No matter how she struggled, she couldn't loose her arm from their grasp.

The bulky person pulled her backwards into the great hall and quietly closed the door behind them with their body. Their mouth was so close to Rosalinde's ear that their lips brushed it as they whispered, "I'm going to release you, Your Highness. If you scream, you'll never make it to the stables."

How did they...

Wait, she recognized that voice. "Romenia?"

"Please, My Queen, keep quiet."

Definitely Romenia, the brawny brute who wielded a sword as if it were her own hand. Relief flooded through Ros at this, though she wasn't sure why. She hadn't seen the woman since she'd escorted Ros and the other mages into the countryside on the hunt for the king. Even then it was going against Rosalinde's commands, as she had dismissed the guards in a bid to protect them and move faster with a smaller company.

She believed Romenia was a servant of Talabrih's throne and she trusted her in a fight, but there was no way of knowing she wasn't bought and paid for by someone else's coin.

Ros shook her head, annoyed at her thoughts. Romenia had been loyal to her family for years, as had many others in the castle that Ros now doubted. She hated feeling like the world had turned against her, but as far as she knew, it had.

"The guards who blocked your way have passed, Queen Rosalinde. I can escort you to the stables now if you'd like."

"How did you know where I was going?" Ros asked.

Though the room was dark, there was enough moonlight coming through the high windows for Ros to see the confusion knitting Romenia's brows. "I am one of the trusted, My Queen. Have you not received the missives sent to your room? Surely everything was explained."

"I've received nothing."

"But Princ—My Queen—I put two of them there myself. One I slipped under your door, the second I delivered when checking for intruders on daily rounds."

Ros shook her head. "There has been no correspondence between myself and...well, anyone."

Romenia clucked her tongue. "This is bad news indeed. We feared there was an enemy among us, but it seems they are closer to you than we suspected if your letters were all stolen."

"Romenia, I'm at a loss. I have no idea what or who you're talking about."

She nodded. "Of course, my apologies."

Ros waited a few seconds in silence before asking, "So, are you going to tell me?"

"Oh, no, I can't. Especially not here. Too many ears about. But perhaps you will learn more on your rendezvous tonight."

Ros looked about the dark, empty room. Too many ears indeed, even in a place where none could be seen. Ros said, "Florian is in on it, then? Whatever *this* is."

Romenia bit her lip, but didn't answer. After a moment, she said, "There are many people involved. More than you think. And though I can't say more, just know that we are with you—guarding you, serving you, protecting the royal house—and we will be ready when you need us. You're not alone, My Queen."

Despite Rosalinde's confusion, she also felt a sense of relief at Romenia's words. She desperately wanted to believe that someone had her back, even if they were slinking through the shadows while she walked in the light.

"Thank you," Ros said, putting as much into those two words as she could without breaking into tears.

"Of course, Your Highness." Romenia peeked out the great hall doors and when she turned back to Ros, her face was lit with a broad smile. "Now let's get you to your tryst."

TRYST WAS NOT a word Ros would have used for meeting Florian, or anyone else for that matter. She and Florian had only become friendly while out searching for her father, when he'd finally had the chance to show who he truly was without the bluster of nobility and his house ambitions. Even that acquaintance had been tempered over the last few weeks while she'd been slinking around with her tail between her legs after being forced to choose a husband she didn't want. Though she truly hoped to build on their budding friendship to make a better Talabrih, she knew that her relationship with Florian would never be more. She wanted to correct Romenia and be certain the woman knew she was not romantically entangled, or any other kind of entangled, with Florian le Fevre.

But Rosalinde's sensibility got the better of her. Romenia was leading her through quiet places, but if correcting her assumption could lead to her getting caught, it was almost better to let Romenia think what she wanted. Or perhaps, what she had been told. Either way, Ros intended to establish the boundaries of their relationship tonight to make sure no one else got the wrong idea about what sort of relationship she had with her new Fire house ambassador.

They reached the stables without incident, though they had to duck out of sight again to avoid another patrol.

Romenia pushed the wide door open to let Ros pass. There was soft lamplight within, reaching warm fingers into the darkness. Ros looked around, but didn't see Florian within.

She turned back to her guard and said, "Thank you for your escort, Romenia."

"My pleasure, Your Highness."

"And just so you know," Ros added, "the Fire mage and I are just friends. This is not a romantic assignation."

Florian emerged from the darkness then, saying, "No need to lie about your feelings, darling. At least, not in front of our most trusted accomplice."

He walked forward and wrapped an arm around Rosalinde's waist. She pushed against him, saying, "Florian, please. I do not wish to be tied to you in such a way."

"How do you want to be tied to me?" he asked, brows raised.

Romenia covered her smile with her hand and said, "My Queen, do not be embarrassed. I am not one to judge the desires of the heart."

"But this isn't—"

"Shhh," Florian whispered, putting a finger against Rosalinde's lips. "Calm down, lover."

Romenia said, "I will guard the area to give you privacy. Take as much time as you need."

"It never takes long, Romenia."

The big woman shook her head. "Then you're doing something wrong."

"Maybe when I'm finished with our Queen, you could give me private lessons."

"I'm not certain you could handle that, Lord le Fevre." With that, Romenia left the stables, pulling the door closed before Ros could further protest. As the darkness gathered around them, leaving them with only gentle flickers of candlelight, Ros called on all her strength and shoved Florian as hard as she could.

"Ow!" he said, rubbing at his ribs.

"What the hell was that?"

Florian laughed. "That was your cover, *sweetums*."

"My cover?"

"Yeah," he said, exasperation clear in his tone. "If you're going to have clandestine meetings in the middle of the night, you have to give people something to talk about so they won't dig into what you're *really* doing."

Rosalinde's brows knit together for a second before she said, "Oh. Right. So, you're not here to try to bed me."

"Don't look so sad about it, Your Highness."

"I'm not sad," she said, straightening to her full height.

"You look very sad. I'm afraid you'll burst into tears at any moment."

"Relieved is more like it. I wasn't sure how you were going to take my rejection of your advances."

Florian shook his head, though a smile still played across his face. "You really thought I would try to bed you, knowing you're in love with someone else? I'm a charming rake, not a scoundrel."

She shrugged. "I thought it might be part of your house's attempts to get closer to the throne."

"Ah, well, I can't argue with that theory. And if I'm being entirely forthright, I did perhaps embellish the level of our intimacy to convince my father to send me back. But that wasn't my idea."

"Whose idea was it?"

"Mine," Elsabet said, stepping from the shadows.

"Elsa? What are you doing here?" Ros asked.

"Saving the kingdom, sis."

"From whom?"

"Everyone. Every*thing*. There's a helluva lot going on right now, moving far faster than I like, and I think it's about time you and I had a chat."

"If that means I get some answers, I agree."

"Ask away, Ros. I'm an open book."

Ros huffed. "Sure you are, but you're written in a language I can't read."

"It isn't as if you've ever tried," Elsa shot back.

"While I hate to interrupt this touching reunion," Florian cut in, "we don't really have time for this. You're on the same side. Act like it."

Elsa gave a terse nod. "Florian's right. Let's get to it."

"You know, that brings up a good question. How did the two of you become allies? From my knowledge of each of you, this seems like an unlikely pairing."

"I've been recruiting those I believe are loyal to the

throne. Florian gave his oath to you and I believed he was sincere."

"Anyone can speak oaths of loyalty," Ros pressed.

Elsa pursed her lips. "Fine. I had him followed until his actions proved him true."

"You what?" Florian asked.

"When I knew he was genuine, I made certain he would stay at the castle indefinitely."

Rosalinde's eyebrows shot up. "Replacing Ambassador Voclain?"

"He'll be fine," Elsa said, waving away the unspoken accusation.

"But the Healers couldn't help him?" Ros asked.

"No one said they *couldn't*," Elsa said. "I just made sure they *didn't*."

"Teague Vannoy," Ros said.

Elsa nodded. "He is in your debt, thanks to a certain conversation you had with his very dear friend Beckett Chastain."

Of course, Ros thought, remembering the night she discovered Teague and Beckett's secret relationship. Both were supposed to be competing for her heart, but she had dismissed the idea entirely when she realized they were in love with one another. She'd promised Beckett a home at the castle so he could stay with Teague, giving his father enough clout at home so that he shouldn't interfere with his son's romantic life.

Ros shot a look toward Florian to gauge his reaction, realizing that Elsa may have just outed her friends. Elsa covered her mouth, realizing what she'd done, but Florian just smiled and said, "Don't worry, I already knew."

"Did they tell you?" Ros asked.

"No," he said. "I'm just observant. They can tell me if they want to, but whether or not they do, I'll keep their secret as long as they wish it. Honestly though, they make such a handsome couple. I hate they feel the need to hide their love."

"Anyway," Elsa said, drawing their attention back to her, "with Teague, Beckett, and Florian on your side, plus those I already knew were committed to you, we had a good foundation to begin the counter-movement."

"Counter-movement to what?"

A flash of confusion crossed Elsa's face before she expertly pushed it away. "Am I to assume you haven't received my letters?"

"No, not one."

"You'd been doing so well avoiding me, like I'd suggested in the letters..." Elsa trailed off. She swallowed, the only indication of her emotion, as she said, "Oh, I see. You weren't sure you could trust me."

Ros felt heat rush to her cheeks as shame filled her. Of course she could trust Elsa, there never should have been a doubt. But there had been. And if she was being honest, there was still mistrust between them even now, and she wasn't sure how to get past it.

"It isn't that I didn't *want* to trust you, I just thought it best if I didn't put my trust in anyone."

Elsa smiled, broader and brighter than Ros had seen in years. "I am so unbelievably proud of you for that."

"Wait...what?"

"You're thinking like a leader, with your head instead of your heart. I can't blame you, after what happened with Mother and the Zoltos."

Mother, Ros thought, letting the word run in one ear and out the other. She couldn't face it. Not now, not yet. There had always been a suspicion in the back of her mind that Queen Sariyah had something to do with the Earth house coup, but she was hesitant to believe she could've done this to her husband of twenty-five years and the father of her children.

Ros couldn't think on that now. There was already so much more to unpack. Luckily, Florian kept her from focusing on her mother's actions by asking, "What *did* happen with the Zoltos? One minute you're in love with the brooding Night house mage, the next you're engaged to the Earth house softy."

"I'm sorry, did you say she's *in love*—you're in *love* with the Night mage?" Elsa asked.

Ros swallowed as her heart fell to her feet. Just thinking about what she did to Cassian, the life she gave up, was enough to make her ill. "Yes, Elsa, I love him."

"I knew you cared for him, but I didn't know the extent," Elsa said. "That must have made things much more difficult when it came to choosing your husband."

Ros said, "In naming my betrothed, I didn't have a choice. I found a letter on my bed, in Larkin Zolto's handwriting, telling me to choose Zandor if I want father returned unharmed."

"And you do?" Florian asked.

"Of course I do!"

He put his hands up and said, "Just checking. His absence landed you a pretty sweet gig. Ruler of Talabrih and all."

"I don't care about that," Ros said. "I mean, I care about our land and our people, but being the queen isn't high on my list of priorities."

Elsa said, "I understand what you're saying, but maybe you need to re-evaluate your list. If you aren't queen, someone else will take over. Choosing from that list of candidates is like trying to decide which color manure to eat—no matter which you choose, they taste the same."

The door pushed open, startling the three of them. Romenia rushed in and said, "Full escort of guards on their way. I couldn't see who they were with."

"Blast," Elsa said. "Romenia, get as far from here as you can. Florian, you know what to do."

Romenia waited not a second more before turning and dashing from the stables. Ros grabbed Elsa's arm and asked, "And what of you?"

"I have to go. I can't be seen with you."

Ros said, "I don't understand."

"I'll explain when I can. For now, just keep playing your role and staying out of trouble. Continue to assume that everyone is your enemy unless I mark them otherwise."

"How will I know?" Ros asked.

Elsa paused for a second, then plucked at the necklace around Rosalinde's throat. It was a dainty thing her father had given her when she turned fifteen, a plain gold necklace bent to look like waves.

"Watch for the rising tide," Elsa said.

With those words, Ros watched her sister disappear into the shadows as smoothly as if she were a Night house master.

Four

ados

Ros turned to Florian. "Where can we hide?"

"In plain sight, Ros," Florian whispered. With a wicked grin, he added, "Forgive me."

He grabbed her then, and for one awful second her memories flashed to Orion Bain; her former friend had gotten handsy one night, and it took a passing bystander to get him off her. *But no, Florian wouldn't do that*, she thought, even as he was pushing her against the wall and his lips were against hers.

The door banged open. Florian jumped away from her in mock surprise when the guards entered the stables. For her part, Ros didn't need to look surprised; indeed, she was still recovering from having Florian's lips dancing along her collarbone.

"Pardon the interruption," the Queen Mother purred, stepping out from her cadre of protectors.

"When I decided to go for a midnight ride, I never anticipated I would happen upon a sight such as this."

"Good thing you *happened* upon us when you did. A few more minutes and your eyes would've gotten a proper show," Florian smirked.

Sariyah pursed her lips. "I am displeased with the way you're presenting yourself to the queen of Talabrih, Lord le Fevre."

"Forgive me, my lady, but you are not the queen I aim to... please."

Ros wanted to smack him for that heavily insinuated pause, but she knew better. After what Elsa had said and the way Florian had jumped into action, Ros knew this had been their plan all along, if something should go wrong. She wasn't sure why they had to impugn her reputation like this—except, she remembered, her reputation had been tarnished years ago.

She felt a smile lift her cheeks at her foolishness. Ros had never been embarrassed about her affairs, had never felt shame for her sexuality. Why should she? But suddenly she had gone from a princess to a queen, and her expectations for how she should behave had changed. Why was she worried about what others thought of her dalliances now, when she was *expected* to find enjoyment outside her marriage bed? Why did she care what anyone expected in the first place? She was the only one who could decide what was acceptable for herself and her body, and anyone who tried to say otherwise could go straight to hell.

"Why are you smiling?" Sariyah hissed. "This is not how the queen should behave."

"Would it be permissible if I gave Florian a room down the hall from my chambers? Perhaps I should arrange vast hunting expeditions like Father, or lengthy diplomatic visits, like you. Florian would happen to be my escort. Those sorts of things are tolerated, are they not?"

Sariyah's eyes were wide as saucers, and it took far longer than normal for her to transform her features into the haughty victim. "Those accusations are baseless."

"Not accusations," Ros said, stepping so close only her mother could hear. "Simply observations. Perhaps I noticed more than you realized through the years."

"I don't know what you think you saw—"

"There's no shame in it, mother, unless you permit it. You're allowed to have a life. You just didn't realize how much of that life I was watching."

Sariyah said, "Clear the room."

The guards about-faced and marched out without hesitation. Florian lingered for a moment, but Ros said, "It's fine. I'll speak with you tomorrow."

He bowed and kissed her hand, gave a perfunctory nod to her mother, and headed for the door. Ros watched him walk away, purposefully checking out his rear to feed into the theater of it all. She found herself pleased with the show, intentionally or not. He turned back once, still seeming unsure about leaving Ros alone with Sariyah, but then he was gone and the two women stood alone, face-to-face.

The Queen Mother's face was unreadable again as she said, "Perhaps you saw more than I gave you credit for. You were always skulking around, though not quite as adeptly as your sister."

Ros felt a venomous response course through her. The weight of it was shocking. She had wanted to call her mother out for years over the way she treated her daughters differently, but she'd never had the guts. Part of her had always felt guilty for even thinking that way, because she loved her mother and her sister, and didn't want to create a rift between them. Somewhere in the back of her mind, she realized her father had always favored her above Elsa, and she wondered if it had hurt Elsa in the same way.

The thought of him sent an ache through Ros. She *missed* him. But now, learning that her mother had played a part in her father's disappearance—though she didn't know the full extent of her role—and in ruining her future marriage with the Night mage, Ros could barely hold her tongue. She wanted to rage at her mother and accuse her of all the secrets that were coming to light, but she knew she couldn't. Elsa needed her to continue to play her role, and that meant keeping quiet about some things. Others though...

"That was something you liked about her, wasn't it? Your own little spy with the innocent mask of a princess. I used to think you liked her better because the two of you were similar, but now I realize it was because of what she could *do* for you as your little pet. How long have you been scheming together, building plans on the whispers Elsa so often hears? Did she send you here tonight to interrupt my fun?"

Sariyah sucked in air between her teeth with a hissing sound. In one sudden revelation, her mask fell away, exposing all the dark emotions she kept hidden under her royal facade. Though she didn't answer Rosalinde's questions, the words she did offer were sharp. "It seems I may have perceived you as more oblivious than you actually are. A slight I will be quick to remedy."

"You've underestimated me my whole life. Why stop now?"

Sariyah smiled, actually *smiled* at Rosalinde's question before walking past Ros and moving to stand in front of one of the Andalusians. She stared at the beast for a moment before glancing over her shoulder and asking, "So tell me, what do you hope to gain from this liaison? Fire house is all but powerless. If you'd gone for an Air house inamorato, I could understand. Now that you've secured Earth house, a pursuit of Air would be strategic, and I could honestly respect you for that. But Florian le Fevre? He's a waste of your time."

"Perhaps I enjoy his company."

"The only person who has ever enjoyed his company is him. Tell the truth: what has he offered you?"

"What power could anyone wield that I don't already have? I *am* the Queen of Talabrih, after all."

Sariyah spun to face her, glaring as she did. "Every queen needs a handful of well-placed pawns, my dear, but you can't retain successful diplomatic relationships if you're bedding all the house-lords' sons."

It was Ros' turn to look surprised. She'd never heard her mother speak in such a way. After a moment, she stammered, "That isn't what this is."

"Oh, of course not. It's *love*, right? That's why you're hiding him in the stables." Sariyah rolled her eyes and said, "Let me give you a piece of advice: choose bedmates who mean nothing. Pick someone of little power, with a family who can be bought, and a personality that will never win you over. They can be easy on the eyes and good in the sack, but never let them be worthy of your heart."

The words were so pointed, so jarringly bitter, that Ros felt a river of pity pouring out for her mother right then. She whispered, "You sound like you're speaking from experience."

"I gave my heart away once, to someone I thought was deserving of it. I was wrong."

Ros bit her lip, afraid to ask the question hammering in her chest. "Was it my father?"

Sariyah met her gaze, her eyes steely and bitter. "I can't see how it matters at this point."

"But it does matter."

"Just take my advice, honey. This isn't a good idea. At least, not right now. You need to focus on your marriage with the Zolto boy until you fulfill your requirements to the kingdom."

"Requirements?" Ros asked.

Sariyah's brows rose. "Women in this kingdom are necessary for one thing."

"You mean children?"

"Of course. You must breed more high caliber Elementalists. After that, you can find yourself a handful of lovers to keep you amused through the years."

"That can't be my whole life. I want more than that, for myself, and for the rest of the women of Talabrih."

"I once thought the same way. I learned my place, and you will too."

"My *place*?" Ros asked. "Mother, you're one of the most talented mages Earth house has ever seen. Your legacy is more than you're giving yourself credit for."

"We can be powerful, and we can be useful, but we are placeholders for powerful men. Even now, while we're regarded as the most powerful women in the land, we'll only hold that power until it gets traded to a king in exchange for peace."

"You speak as though we're at war and in need of rescue."

Sariyah sighed. "That's what life is, darling. One little war after another. Choose which battles are worth fighting and let the others pass you by."

Ros couldn't believe what she was hearing. She'd thought her mother content, if not happy. Now it sounded as if she'd had a miserable life and expected her daughter to do the same.

"I'm sorry your life hasn't turned out the way you wanted it to," Ros said. "I wish you'd had something better, something good and hopeful, that you could have passed on to your daughters. More than that, I'm sorry your days have turned you into this wretched shell of the woman I thought I knew. But I will not give up and let my life become the same sort of mess out of a sense of duty. I will not allow my existence to be so dismal just because you did."

Ros turned to walk out of the barn, but her mother called out, "That's what I thought, too, when your grandmother gave me this same talk. No one thinks their life will turn out like this. Every fool believes they're the one to change things for the better."

Without turning back to her, Ros said, "You're not dead yet, Sariyah. There's still time to make your life count for something."

Ros walked out of the stables feeling like she'd just watched her entire world burn.

Five

Ros didn't see Elsa, Florian, or her mother for the next two days. She hadn't been trying to avoid them, but perhaps they were steering clear of her after their adventures in the stables. Of the three, it was actually Florian she was the most hesitant to see. She knew he'd only been doing what he had to do to keep their secrets, but every time she caught sight of someone with the same golden hair, heat crept up her neck, lingering on the spots his lips had touched.

She shamed herself every time this happened. There was no doubt in her heart that she was in love with Cassian, but it wasn't her heart that needed reminding. No, it was the involuntary bodily response to Florian that had to be shunned, and she was rebuffing herself with disconcerting regularity.

Early on the third day, a vicious thudding on her

bedroom door gave Ros a bit of distraction. She rose from the chair where she'd been reading to find a young woman with short black hair and a dull gray cloak standing breathless in the hall.

"Hello," Ros said, squinting slightly at the girl. She didn't recognize her, which in itself was strange, as she tended to know everyone who had access to the royal apartments.

"Forgive the intrusion," the girl said, dipping into an unpracticed bow.

A bow, Ros thought. *Not a curtsy. How peculiar.*

The girl looked back over her shoulder as if she was expecting someone to charge at her at any moment. She turned back to Ros and flipped the inside hem of her cloak up. Upon it was a hastily stitched wave.

Ros whispered, "The rising tide."

The girl nodded. "There's trouble in the courtyard. Your friends need you."

"What's going on?" Ros asked.

The girl glanced over her shoulder again. "No time, Highness. Trust the tide."

"Right," Ros said. She grabbed a robe from the edge of the bed and tossed it over her shoulders. When she turned back to the door, the girl was gone. Ros took a deep breath, closed her bedroom door behind her, and muttered, "Trust the tide."

She heard the commotion long before she reached the courtyard. There were clumps of servants scattered in the hallways trying to see what was happening, though as soon as they saw Queen Rosalinde approaching, all miraculously remembered an important aspect of their jobs that needed done. Ros paid no attention to them—her eyes were on the man kneeling in the middle of the courtyard.

Ros swooped out from the cover of the stone archway, the crowd parting for her as she approached. She reached the kneeling man and stopped short as she realized who he was.

"Beckett?" she asked.

She spun toward the figures standing on the steps to her right. "What is the meaning of this?"

The Zolto siblings looked down at her. Zandor wore a chastised look, wincing as if he was participating in something that gave no pleasure.

Then there was his sister.

Larkin's face was shockingly sweet, taking on a wounded look at Rosalinde's question. Her hand flew to her chest as she asked, "Whatever do you mean?"

Ros felt as if her blood was boiling inside her. For Larkin to be so callous when there was a kind young man crying on the ground in front of her...it sent a spear of rage right through her. She opened her mouth to speak, but caught sight of a smirking Queen Mother just off to the side of the courtyard. Was she behind this as well?

Taking a cue from her mother, Ros took a steadying breath and cleared her face of emotion, or at least, as much as she could. She'd never been as good at it as her mother or sister, but she could manage it well enough, especially after weeks of trying to disguise her boredom while listening to the nobles' squabbles.

"Pray tell," Ros said, her voice as cold as she could make it, "why is this gentlefellow on the cold ground before you? Our noble brother deserves better than that."

Larkin took on a look of pity as she said, "Our good friend here received some news that has upset him, but it's nothing to worry your royal head about."

"My royal head will not rest when I see my people hurting."

Beckett looked up then, seeming to just now realize that Ros was there. "My Queen, please. Don't let them do this."

Ros stepped closer and reached her hand down to rest on his shoulder. She said, "What has happened?"

"My father..." he muttered before breaking down in tears again.

"Lord Chastain has called for his son to be returned to their home," Larkin cut in. "There is no need for these theatrics."

"He's forcing me to marry," Beckett said.

Ros inhaled sharply. She knew what it meant for him to go home, to be forced away from Teague, and she had promised he could stay as long as he wished under her protection.

"It is unfortunate we must deny his request. His son does not wish to return," Ros replied.

"Beckett Chastain will return to his father's home at once," Larkin said. "There is no refusing this request."

"It is not your decision to make. He is of age and can choose to stay or go as he desires."

"Of age or not, he is a mage of Earth house and will be dealt with as we see fit."

"Dealt with? Is he charged with a crime? Has he committed some heinous act I'm unaware of? Or are we simply denying people their autonomy because we think we can?"

"He belongs at home, Ros."

The crowd gasped at Larkin's use of Rosalinde's nickname, shocked that she would speak to the Queen of Talabrih in such an informal way. Rosalinde's brows rose and she gave a small smile—not to Larkin, but to her mother. She hadn't trained her mouthpiece as well as she thought.

"Forgive me, Your Majesty," Larkin ground out through clenched teeth. "I spoke out of turn. My passion exceeded my sense."

Rosalinde waved away her words, a magnanimous gesture in the crowd's eyes. "Understandable. You want to do right by your house lord. I want to do right by his son. And if you were in your own home, perhaps this would be a different conversation. But you are not. You are in *my* home, and I am the authority of the land, including Earth house and any disputes that arise. So when I say this young man may do as he wishes, you are wasting your breath to say otherwise."

The women looked at each other, a silent war waging between them. There was a flicker of something in her eyes—guilt, maybe—but then she hardened her expression against Rosalinde's stare. Ros knew Larkin through and through, or at least she had thought she did, but this look was something she'd never seen, a cruelty that had not been there through their many years of friendship.

But it *was* something she recognized. She'd seen it a few nights before in the stables when she'd spoken to her mother. It hadn't occurred to her then to question her mother's harsh words, for though they hadn't sounded like the woman she'd known all her life, the emotion behind them had felt too raw to attribute to anything other than a life of pain.

Now, though, she could see, or thought she could anyway, that it was more than that. It was an amplification of every slight, every hurt, every cruelty that had ever been part of these women's lives. Ros couldn't be certain, but for a brief second, she thought she saw a flicker of darkness flit through Larkin's eyes.

They were infected.

Ros wasn't sure what had happened to Gaius in those woods after Cassian brought her back to the castle, but at least part of him still survived. It lingered inside the people closest to Rosalinde, turning the tiny darkness that was already there into a monster that she couldn't control.

Though she wasn't sure how she could possibly defeat it, she knew she had to start here, in front of the assembled people. She needed them to believe in her.

"Rise, Beckett Chastain. Your home is here now. You will live and work in the castle at my discretion and no one else's."

"Lord Chastain will not be pleased," Larkin said.

"Have him send word through his ambassador."

She smirked. "*I* am his ambassador."

Ros knew she meant the words to shock her. Her father's Earth house ambassador was a kind, elderly man who had been there for years. Larkin must've replaced him in secret through less than scrupulous means.

Still, Ros didn't let her surprise show. Without missing a beat, she said, "Not anymore. Beckett Chastain will now report to me for Earth house. I doubt his father will be able to sway him to his request."

"You can't do that," Larkin said.

"Mind your tongue," Ros spat. "You have no power here aside from what I give. Return to Earth house on your own or I will have you escorted by the royal guards."

There was a hushed silence over the crowd. Quiet as a pin drop, Zandor said, "Please, don't do this."

"I will protect my people, *beloved*, even if that means making unpopular decisions. I suggest you learn this lesson well, or you may find yourself on your way home to Earth house, too."

Ros turned and marched from the courtyard, Beckett Chastain in tow. Not a single eye drifted her way. She was certain there would be whispers and rumors within seconds of her clearing the area, but she couldn't worry about what they said. She'd made a promise to Beckett nearly a month ago, and she planned to keep it.

Once they were out of earshot of the crowd, she whispered, "Where have you been sleeping?"

Beckett looked surprised by the question. He puffed out his breath, and with a still-shaky voice, he said, "Teague's quarters."

Of course. Why had she even asked? Still...

"It might be best if you find somewhere else to sleep for a few days, at least until this whole thing passes. I'm certain there's an empty room in the visitor's wing."

"I have a room," Beckett said, "but I haven't been using it."

"Use it now. I'm not sure how your house lords will respond, and I'd rather keep Teague out of this, if possible."

"As would I," he said. While they walked, a smile spread across his face. "That was quite a display back there. No one has ever challenged another house's authority so openly."

"They overreach, thinking the crown is weak, that they retain more power than they do and that now is the perfect time to gather more about them while there's a new ruler on the throne. I've done nothing to dissuade that line of thinking."

"Until today."

She nodded. "They'll disregard it as a temper tantrum or a sign of affection between us. Within the next few days, they are likely to push back."

"What can they do against the queen?" he asked.

Ros bit her lip. There was a *lot* they could do against her, including removing her like they had her father. But she didn't say that to Beckett. He had been so afraid only minutes before, and she didn't want to make him worry even more.

"Hard to say what they might try," she said, hoping her voice sounded more confident than she felt. "Whatever it is, we'll be ready for it."

THERE WERE four guards waiting outside Rosalinde's bedroom when she returned.

"Good day, Your Highness," one of them said.

She looked them over, trying to gauge the situation. She only recognized the one who spoke, so the others were probably recent additions from the Zolto forces.

"Leeza," Ros said, nodding toward the woman. "Good to see you. How's the new baby?"

Leeza seemed surprised by the question, but replied, "She's good. Cries a lot, but that's expected."

"And your wife is recovering well, aside from not getting enough sleep?"

Before Leeza could respond, one of the unknown guards said, "If you could come with us, Queen Rosalinde."

She sized up the man in front of her. He was older than the rest, silver creeping into his hair at his temples and a thick shock of it in his beard. She counted three scars on him with just a quick once over, so there were probably more in places she couldn't see, indicating he'd seen more action than the younger three. He was muscled, but not bulky; fit, but not consumed by staying in shape. This was a man who knew how to intimidate with his presence, but could throw down if he needed to.

Ros chewed the inside of her cheek for a moment, weighing her options. Finally, she asked, "And what if I choose not to?"

"Let's hope it doesn't come to that."

At his threat, she felt her gift rushing to her fingertips, begging to be used. She could take them out with a flick of her wrist, but she didn't want to hurt them if she didn't have to. Besides, she needed to find out why they were there in the first place.

"Perhaps you could simply tell me what's going on and I'll go willingly."

"It isn't our job to know what's going on, it's our job to get you there. And they have advised us to take you by any means necessary."

Everything inside her screamed for her to run, but she couldn't. She wouldn't. Whatever was happening, she needed to play her part. If not for herself, then to protect the others who were counting on her, like Florian, Elsa, and whoever else was involved with the rising tide.

"While I don't appreciate the way you're behaving, I shall acquiesce to your request. Lead the way."

Six

She expected them to take her to the great hall. Many informal meetings and conversations took place there, so it was the most natural choice of location. Instead, she found herself standing in front of the doors to the throne room. She stared up at the gilded crests upon them, suddenly less sure of what was about to happen and more nervous than the Queen of Talabrih should be.

Then again, maybe this was one part of being a ruler that she wasn't aware of. Perhaps her father had felt this way every day and she'd never been privy to those private, nervous thoughts. The throne room was the most important place in all of Talabrih, where laws were proclaimed and justice was served; feeling awe and a little fear was natural. Or at least that's what she kept telling herself.

Ros rubbed her hands down the sides of her robe. She would have demanded the time to change into something more suitable had she known this was their destination. The last thing she wanted to do was step into the throne room without *looking* like the Queen of Talabrih, even if she didn't feel like a queen at that moment. As it were, her lounging dress and long robe would have to do.

The guards pushed open the doors and Ros walked forward toward the throne. It sat empty before her, and something about that fact surprised her. Part of her had expected to see Larkin there, or maybe her mother. Although she did not know what she would have said or done if one of them was there, she was equally unprepared for the massive, vacant chair that seemed to taunt her with its emptiness.

There were smaller chairs set up in front of the dais, one for each of the houses. To the far left sat Hessian Barclay of Air house, his arms folded across his chest. Beside him was Florian's father, Gilthroy le Fevre. They'd left the middle chair open for Ros, the Water house representative, and beside her was Lady Valeria Auguste of Earth house. The fifth and final seat was empty and had always been so. It was the seat left open for Night house.

Ros walked forward, stopping a few feet in front of the house rulers. She said nothing, refusing to give them the satisfaction. Though she wasn't sure why she was here or what they had to say, she could tell by the way Barclay's face was practically beaming that it was bad news for her.

After a moment that seemed to stretch for an

awkward length of time, Lady Auguste finally stood, smoothed down her gown, and said, "You stand accused of demeaning the crown and the position that holds it, mental instability, and tyrannical use of power. How do you plead?"

The words struck as forcefully as if someone had slapped her. Ros stammered, "Not guilty."

"We have witness statements from numerous people present in the courtyard today, as well as firsthand accounts of multiple other encounters. Do you refute the words of dozens of people all reporting the same thing?" Barclay asked.

"I kept a scared young man from going home. He clearly did not wish to go, and since he is of age, he should have a say in what becomes of him. I see no issue with that," Ros said.

"Why would you interfere in such a matter?" Valeria asked. "Shouldn't the decision fall to the house ruler, or the ambassador in her stead?"

"The ambassador was openly hostile toward the man and the throne, giving no indication he would be treated fairly if left to the Earth house representative."

Valeria asked, "Is that why you dismissed her and tried to replace her with the same man she was sending home at the request of his father?"

Before Ros could answer, the Fire house lord tutted and said, "You cannot do that, nor should you want to. We have the right to choose the ambassadors, not you. To keep up the sanctity of the throne and stabilize the remaining houses, we must be able to choose who represents us. In all my years, I've never heard of such a thing, even by a ruler as inexperienced as you."

Ros remembered that Gilthroy had been returning to Fire house and sent Florian back as ambassador. So how had the house ruler appeared so suddenly after the encounter, considering not even two hours had passed since the issue between Beckett and Larkin?

"What are the Fire house prerequisites to be an ambassador?" Ros asked. "Do you have any? Or do you give the position to whomever you think is most likely to bed the crown?"

Gilthroy's eyes went wide, but it was an entirely different voice that spoke, one she knew well: her mother. "Is that why you appointed the Chastain boy over your best friend? Already bored with bedding the one Gilthroy sent you, so you chose a new one from Earth house and didn't want to risk them taking away your toy?"

"Hello, Mother. I'm surprised you had time to make an appearance, what, with all the trouble you've been causing."

"I always make time for the kingdom, darling, especially when it's in danger."

"You think I'm a danger to the kingdom?" Ros asked, a laugh escaping her. "Is that what happened to Father? You thought he was a danger, so you had him removed."

"How dare you hurl such a baseless accusation at me?

58

I *loved* that man. I would never want to harm him. Everyone in the kingdom knows how strong our bond is."

"I don't know what you did, but I know you're lying. You had something to do with getting rid of him. I'll figure out a way to prove it."

"Actually, sister," Elsabet said as she walked up the aisle to stand beside Sariyah, "after extensive investigations, I believe the real culprit was you."

A well of sorrow opened in Rosalinde's chest. "Oh, Elsa, not you, too."

"Yes, me, Usurper Queen. I stand on the side of truth."

"I would never hurt our father," Ros said, her voice barely a whisper now.

Elsa ignored her, saying, "You were tired of waiting to take over the kingdom, tired of his will being imposed on you. When he told you who you should marry, that was the last straw. You knew no one would suspect you, the grieving daughter. Once he was out of the way, you could go forward with your plans to marry that nefarious Night house mage and take the throne."

"None of this is true."

Ros searched Elsa's eyes, certain she would find the darkness slithering through them, but there was no trace of it. But if Elsa wasn't infected with the darkness, then these words were hers. She couldn't blame a shadowy figure for the rift between them; she'd done that all on her own. Now it grew into a chasm that couldn't be mended.

"Of course, your best friend, Larkin Zolto, grew suspicious of what was happening. To throw her off, you chose her brother as your betrothed and sent the Night house mage away. Or killed him. With someone as devious as you, it's hard to say."

"This is absurd," Ros said.

Her voice sounded wrong in her ears, too high, nearly strangled. She couldn't believe she had to defend herself against such outrageous lies. She loved her father and had no desire to take Talabrih from him. Ros didn't even want to be queen. Elsa *knew* that.

"What's absurd is that you almost got away with it. Thankfully, there's a *tide* of people who will never let the kingdom fall into evil hands. We will protect this kingdom with our every breath."

Rosalinde's gaze jerked to her sister's, trying to confirm there was an underlying message. She'd give the world to know that Elsa hadn't moved against her. She tried to understand what she saw there, to read past the words to the heart of who her sister was, but they'd never had that sort of relationship. Ros could read into what Larkin was thinking with just a glance, but she'd never put in the work to understand her younger sister.

"There's only one thing that can be done," the Queen Mother said. "A vote of no confidence."

"You'd need a majority to remove her from the throne," Gilthroy said. "And I don't think you have it."

Lady Auguste's brows furrowed. "A reprimand, surely, but to remove her? It seems hasty."

"You have my vote," Air house said.

Florian's father shook his head. "I cannot abide by this decision without due process. If Queen Rosalinde is truly guilty, we should remove her from her throne and punished for her actions. But as of now, we have a young ruler making an error with no proof of a deeper nefarious plot. I will not vote for this until the accusations are verified."

Elsa said, "Lady Auguste, I may be of Water house because of my father, but my gift lies with Earth. I will honor you in my rule, and I will hold the oath my sister made and marry an Earth house mage, if you agree to remove my sister and put me on the throne."

The Earth house ruler looked at Elsa, shaking her head. "This can't be our only option. You're barely seventeen."

"You are the youngest house ruler in history," Elsa said. "Yet you have made Earth house a shining jewel in Talabrih's crown. Age does not equate intelligence or adequacy."

The woman let out a long, heavy sigh. "Be that as it may, I hold a heavy heart in this decision."

"That's only natural," Sariyah said. "You are your mother's daughter. She had such a kindness about her, a heart that bled for Talabrih. She would be conflicted now as well, but I know she would've made the right decision for the kingdom."

Auguste swallowed. "I forgot you were friends."

"The best of friends," Sariyah said. "We grew together, planted our roots deep in Earth house, in Talabrih. From our roots, you've nurtured Earth house into a blossoming tree, providing for our people. You are wise, and I trust you to know the right decision in this."

With a nod, Auguste said, "You have the vote of Earth house."

"Two yes and one no is still a majority," Sariyah said.

"I vote no," Ros said, defiance clear on her face. "As I am still the ruler of Water house, my vote joins with Fire house to negate the others."

"It seems we are at an impasse," Elsa said.

"Or we would be, if I weren't here."

The voice purred through the room, silky and deep. Ros felt it ooze over her, filling her with dread. She'd never heard it fully alive, only the remnants of it, but now here he was in the flesh: Gaius Scalise.

For the briefest moment when he'd first spoken, she had thought it was Cassian. She'd thought he was there to save her, to rescue her from whatever trap had been laid, but no, not this time. She'd quickly realized it wasn't her savior who'd come, but her demise. Though the brothers had the same timbre, Cassian's voice didn't have the bitter edge that Gaius' did.

Ros did not know how he had transformed from the disembodied darkness to the man standing before her, but he *was* standing there, a tall, lithe figure in black. His head was shaved, his cheeks sunken. His eyes were nothing more than deep, black pools.

"And who might you be?" Gilthroy le Fevre asked.

"I'm surprised you don't remember me, Gil," Gaius said. "You were always kind to me when you visited my mother. You brought me toys and gifts for years, and when my mother bore you a son, I dreamed we might all be one big happy family. Alas, that isn't what happened, but you can't blame a child for having hope."

A son? Ros thought. *Gilthroy le Fevre was Cassian's father? Did Florian know he had a brother? Did Cassian?*

The Fire house ruler's eyes grew unbelievably large, and he said, "No, it can't be."

"That's right. You remember, don't you? Gaius Scalise, in the flesh," he said, darting a look to Ros. "The sole member of Night house."

"Sole member?" Hessian Barclay asked. "What about the one who competed in the Great Match?"

Gaius met Rosalinde's gaze and sneered. "My brother is dead. As is my poor mother. But don't fret; I'm here now, and I'm far superior to the few Night mages you've dealt with in the past. Far more powerful, as well."

The house rulers cast furtive glances to one another as Gaius moved around the table and sat down in the empty Night house seat.

Gilthroy said, "Listen, son—"

"No. I am not your son. You made that perfectly clear when I was eight and tried to hug the man who'd been visiting off and on for years, only to be pushed away like I was mud on your boots." Gaius stared down Gilthroy until the older man averted his eyes. "So you listen, old man, and take note. Night house will no longer be the silent secret that plagues your nightmares. I will not allow it anymore. This seat has sat open long enough."

There was silence for a moment, but finally Barclay said, "Night house, the Queen of Talabrih stands accused of impropriety regarding her use of power. Two of the four of us have voted to remove her from the throne. What is your vote?"

Gaius smiled wickedly and said, "Night house breaks the tie with a vote of no confidence. The queen is dead. Long live the queen."

Seven

S trong hands gripped Rosalinde's arms. They pulled her from the throne room, practically dragging her, but her eyes never left Gaius and his smile never faltered. There was nothing in the entire world that mattered to her right then, not her safety, not her family and their deceit, not even her beloved kingdom. Gaius had said his brother was dead. *Cassian* was dead.

At that moment, Ros didn't care what happened. She could spend the rest of her life in a cell or her days could end tomorrow. Either way, she'd never get a chance to make things right with the man she loved.

"What in the overworld is wrong with you? Open the door."

The words filtered down through her haze and she realized they were already at the entrance to the dungeon.

She hadn't noticed their many steps to get there, lost in misery at the thought of a world without Cassian.

"Terribly sorry, old chap. I was just surprised to see the queen in your custody."

"She's not the queen anymore," the guard holding her said.

"Is that right? What an unexpected turn of events."

Ros knew that voice. But it wasn't the voice of a guard. The cadence of the words, the lilting way he spoke, it was all wrong.

They stepped through the door and took two steps down toward the cells when the guards suddenly came to a halt. Ros looked up to see why they'd stopped, when there on the steps was the fiercest woman Ros had ever seen. Sword drawn in front of her, she looked like a statue of warriors past. Her long blonde braid swung back and forth and she readied her stance.

"You'll not take her any further," Romenia said.

One guard laughed, though Ros wasn't sure how anyone could be so daring when staring at the point of Romenia's sword.

The other guard said, "You dolt. There are two of us, and we've got the high ground."

"Um, actually no," said the same lilting voice behind them. "*I* have the high ground."

Ros flinched as a lightning bolt shot straight through the face of the guard who had just spoken. The laughing guard tried to push Ros back up the steps in front of him as cover, but Romenia's sword was through his gut half a second later.

Florian pulled off the helmet he'd been wearing while pretending to be the dungeon guard. "All right, Highness?"

Ros nodded. "Yes, but you don't need to call me that anymore. I am no longer the queen."

"Bollocks," Romenia said. Her eyes went wide and she said, "Forgive my language, Your Highness, but you will always be the true queen, even if someone else wears the crown."

Ros gave Romenia's firm shoulder a squeeze. She was grateful for the woman's loyalty and proud to have her as an ally. "How did you know they'd bring me here?"

"A runner," Florian said. "They found Romenia, and she found me."

Ros asked, "A girl with short black hair?"

Romenia nodded. "Told me this was our only chance to get you out. Once you made it to the cells, it was over. Seemed very confident of that, too."

"Speaking of 'over,' what happens next?" Florian asked. "I was never quite clear about the rest of our plan. How do we get out of here?"

Romenia winced. "Honestly, this is the extent I planned. I didn't expect to make it this far."

"No? Not even with the help of a handsome, debonair mage like myself?"

"I thought you'd be dead by now," Romenia said.

He smirked. "But we just got started."

"I know."

The door above them opened, and Romenia pushed Ros behind her, readying her sword. Beckett stood framed in the light from the hall. He held his hands up and said, "Whoa, just me."

"What are you doing here?" Ros said. "I told you to lie low."

"Right, but then you went and got yourself deposed. Besides, I'm just doing what I was told. Your runner found me a good hiding place to keep watch on the dungeon and said to open this door two minutes after you went in."

Runner. Who was that girl? And how did she know so much?

"Then what?" Romenia asked.

Beckett smiled. "A daring escape."

Florian, Ros, and Romenia followed Beckett back into the hall. They ducked into the dark, dusty room where the runner had instructed Beckett to wait and snuck through a hidden side door that was connected to it, emerging in the hall that led to the library.

"This is a dead end," Ros whispered.

"Trust the Rising Tide," a voice said from the shadows. The runner girl stepped out in front of them, seeming to appear from the dark itself.

"Who are you?" Ros asked.

"A mutual friend asked me to keep an eye on you," she said. "Though honestly, I've had to use both. You get yourself in a lot of trouble."

Ros pursed her lips. "What friend?"

"Do you want to have this discussion now, here, or could it wait until people aren't chasing you?" she asked.

"It can wait," Florian said. "Get us out of here."

The girl headed into the library. Though they all followed, Ros knew for certain there was no way out. She had scoured the place thoroughly when she was younger, playing hide-and-find with Elsa, or as a teenager looking for a suitable spot for snogging. Neither attempt had been fruitful. She could "trust the Rising Tide" and still not want to be backed into a corner.

The runner led them to the center of the room where plush armchairs surrounded a large ornate table. It was supposed to be a place for the house rulers to gather to discuss issues or for the scholars to debate whatever they debated, but Ros had never seen it used.

Nimble as a cat, the runner slid under the table and pulled aside the carpet underneath, revealing a trapdoor. "I'll need a hand, Beckett."

Beckett climbed under with her, but she already had the door open before he reached her. She mumbled something to him, and a few seconds later, Beckett disappeared into the darkness.

"What's happening?" Ros asked.

The girl looked over her shoulder, a smirk on her face. "You have some real trust issues, don't you?"

"I don't know you," Ros said.

"I don't know you, either," the girl replied, "but I'm risking my rear to save yours. So how about you settle down with the questions and let me focus on getting everyone out of here?"

Ros huffed. "At least tell me your name."

The girl looked as if she would answer, but the thud of boots running down the hallway cut off anything she might say. The girl grabbed Rosalinde's hand and pulled her under the table. Ros looked back to see Romenia with her sword out and Florian standing behind her, hands outstretched as lightning crackled along his hands and up his forearms.

"Go," Romenia said. "We'll hold them off."

"No," Florian replied, pushing against Romenia's shoulder. "You go with the Queen. I'll handle this."

"What if you can't?" Ros asked.

"Then I'll flirt with them until they're putty in my hands. Either way, you need to go," Florian said.

"I'm serious."

"So am I. My father is the leader of Fire house, but I can still pretend I didn't know what was happening."

"They'll know you're lying," Ros said.

"Then I'll tell them your brutish guard threatened my life."

"Much more believable," Romenia said.

Florian flashed Romenia a grin. "Or maybe I was bewitched by your beauty, unable to help myself. Then I won't be lying."

Ros barely had time to register the blush on Romenia's cheeks before the guard grabbed Ros by the waist to pull her into the trapdoor.

Ros yelled, "No, I'm not leaving him."

"Yes, you are," the runner said, pushing Ros down into the hole.

She fell for only a second before landing on something soft and springy. As Romenia climbed down after them and closed the trapdoor above, it was too dark to see what it was, but she heard Beckett say, "You're welcome."

"Is the ladder ready?" the runner asked.

"Yes," Beckett said.

"Then why aren't you down it?"

The girl struck a match and lit a small lamp, illuminating their faces and casting long shadows through the strange room. It was a narrow area with low ceilings. Though Beckett was hunched over, his back still rubbed against the ceiling. The walls were stone, slick with dripping water and moss.

"I wanted to wait for you," Beckett said. "Where's Florian?"

Ros said, "Still in the library. We can still save him."

"He's giving us a chance to get out. We need to take it," the runner said.

The girl pushed past Beckett and headed down the corridor, her lantern bobbing ahead of them. Ros cast a look up at the trapdoor overhead. She desperately wanted to go back for Florian.

"He wants you to keep going, Your Highness," Romenia said. "He believes in you."

"He's risking his life..."

"He knows the risk. He did it anyway."

Ros could barely see the woman's face now as the runner's lamp faded in the distance. "Okay, let's go then. You first."

"I hope you didn't really expect that to work. If so, we may have miscalculated our faith in you, My Queen."

A laugh escaped Rosalinde despite herself. "Fine, but from here on out, you need to drop the titles. I'm Ros. Just Ros."

"As you say."

Ros climbed down from the soft leaves that Beckett had used to catch her. She hunched over and chased after the last bit of light she could see ahead of her. When she and Romenia finally caught up, she found the runner standing at the edge of an overhang. It was a small place created where one of the drum towers met the wall, and as many times as Ros had walked around the castle looking for ways to sneak in and out, she knew it was invisible from the outside. The shadowed corner of the drum tower and the wall hid this exit perfectly.

"Where's Beckett?" Romenia asked.

The runner pointed down. Ros looked over the edge of the opening to see Beckett climbing down a trellis formed from vines. He had clearly done good work with his Botanical gift and was near the bottom now.

"You next, soldier," the runner said.

"I stay with the Queen."

The runner rubbed at her temples, mumbling, "I can't believe I let him talk me into this." Then louder, she said, "Climb down now. If guards get down there before her, she'll need help to defend herself."

"And if they come this way before she's down?"

"Then I'll take care of it."

"How?" Ros asked.

"Can't a girl keep some secrets of her own?"

The words jarred something inside Ros. She'd heard a similar question while standing in the stables with Cassian Scalise, in the last moment before she knew her father was actually missing, before her world went sideways.

Ros looked at Romenia and said, "Go. I'm right behind you."

Romenia didn't question further, simply began her descent. Once she was out of earshot, Ros spun on the runner. "Tell me who you are."

"I told you already—"

"Did Cassian send you?"

The girl paused, her eyes trailing up Rosalinde's face to meet her eyes. The look she gave her startled Ros, as she hadn't noticed the strange silver-gray of her eyes before. Being caught in that stare was haunting.

"Yes."

"Is he okay? Alive?"

"I don't know. He was, last time I saw him."

A small part of Ros' heart unclenched just a bit. Gaius hadn't killed him during their fight in the woods. He'd been at the naming ceremony, after all. At some point between then and now, he'd sent this girl to the castle to look out for her. There was a chance Gaius had been lying—that was what he *did*—and that chance was enough for now.

"Climb down, Highness."

"I'm not the Queen any longer. Call me Ros."

The girl nodded. "Brisa Delos Santos."

"But the Delos Santos name died off years ago"

"Almost."

"They were the original..." Ros trailed off. She looked at the smirking girl in front of her as it all clicked into place.

"That's right, *Ros*. The last descendent of the original royal family. Pretty sure that makes me the true Queen."

Ros gaped at the girl, unsure what to say. If she really was a Delos Santos, why was she running around in forgotten passages with a deposed ruler rather than taking the crown for herself? All knew the original royal family; they were the stuff of legends. If a missing descendent appeared, the houses would place her on the throne without question.

After her stunned silence, Ros finally managed to say, "I don't understand."

"Halt!" a guard yelled.

They'd found the passage. What that meant for Florian, Ros wasn't sure. What it meant for them...

Before Ros could react, Brisa sprang into action. She smashed her lantern on the ground, leaving them in shadow. Putting her arm around Rosalinde's waist, Brisa said, "Hold on," and took a step.

Their feet left the floor of the corridor and landed on soft grass. Ros said, "You're a Night mage."

"Sort of," the girl smirked. Then, brows furrowed, she asked, "How did you think I knew Cassian?"

Without warning, Brisa's knees buckled, and she tumbled to her hands and knees. Ros kneeled at her side, saying, "Are you hurt?"

Brisa shook her head. "Just weak. I'm not great at making jumps like that, and worse when I'm transporting someone with me."

"Cassian made it seem so simple."

Brisa smiled. "Cas is a showoff."

Romenia and Beckett were at their sides a minute later. Romenia immediately started checking Ros for injury. Ros waved her away and said, "I'm fine. It's Brisa who needs help."

The Night mage huffed. "I'll be okay. I just need a few minutes to rest."

"We don't have a few minutes," Beckett said, pointing to the castle doors that were opening.

"We need to scatter," Brisa said.

"You can barely move," Ros countered.

"Go on without me. I can get away from the guards after I've recovered. We'll rendezvous at the place I told you about."

Romenia and Beckett nodded, but Ros didn't know what they were talking about. Romenia pulled on Rosalinde's arm, trying to get her to leave the fallen Elementalist.

"No," Ros said. "We can't leave someone else."

Brisa ignored Ros, looking instead to Romenia. "Get her out of here."

Romenia didn't hesitate. She grabbed Ros by the waist and threw the former queen over her broad shoulders. Romenia ran across the meadow, straight for the forest beyond. Ros bobbed against her back, struggling and failing to get out of the woman's grasp. She stared after the place where Brisa had been, but couldn't pick her out in the waning light of dusk.

They moved under the cover of the trees, where no light passed through the thick canopy above. Romenia stumbled twice before finally agreeing to Rosalinde's protests to put her down.

Standing on her own feet, Ros looked around and asked, "Where's Beckett?"

"No idea," Romenia said. "Our plan was always to split up and find our way to the rendezvous point two nights from now."

"Is that still the plan?"

There was a crackle of leaves behind them and Romenia swung around, drawing her sword as she did. In a whisper so soft Ros wasn't sure she'd actually spoken, Romenia said, "Get behind me. Slowly."

Ros did as she was instructed, her eyes straining to look through the forest as she did so. It was too dark to see more than a few feet away from them, and Ros felt far too exposed.

They stood there in the quiet for hours, it seemed,

though Ros was sure it had really only been a couple minutes. She was about to suggest they move on when the unmistakable whistle of blades being drawn filled the surrounding air.

"Go north," Romenia said. "Find somewhere to hide during the day. The Tide will come for you."

"What? No," Ros said.

"On the count of three, you run as hard and as fast as you can and you don't look back."

"I can fight."

"One."

"I can use my magic."

"Two."

"Romenia, please—"

"Three," the woman roared.

She charged into the darkness, and Ros heard the clang of metal meeting metal. Ros knew she should do as Romenia said. They had all been putting their lives on the line for hers, but why? She was nothing special. Well, she wouldn't let Romenia die for her. She could call on her powers and help her.

Ros took a step toward where Romenia had gone, but as she did, a hulking, blood-soaked guard barreled at her from out of the darkness. Ros jumped back as he dived toward her. She sidestepped him as he scrambled to grab hold of her. Another guard burst through the trees and lumbered toward her. She reached for her magic, willing it to her fingers, but the spark in her fell still before she could call it out.

Panic filled her. She'd used her powers to fight before, so why were they abandoning her now? She did the only thing she knew to do—she ran.

The trees were a blur as she darted through the forest. She could hear someone behind her, cursing at every errant branch or thorn that scratched their face. Ros did not know if she was going the right way. All she knew was she had to get away. There was shame in running, in knowing her friends had stood their ground, maybe even died, just so she could run. But she couldn't deal with the shame right now. She knew she'd feel it for a long time if she made it out of there.

In Rosalinde's mind, she could see the guards directly behind her, feel the slice of their swords as they brought them down on her. She couldn't shake the feeling that they were right on her heels. Venturing a look behind her, she couldn't see anything in the dark. She turned back around just in time to run face first into a tree.

Ros fell. She shook away the daze from hitting the tree—no, wait, that was *not* a tree. It was a man. A tall man, with sandy brown hair and hazel eyes. A man she could have loved if things in her life were different, if she was not a royal.

"Rosa?" Alaric asked. "Are you okay?"

He helped her stand. She tried to answer him, but couldn't find the words to say, *No, I'm not okay. Guards are chasing me, I've been deposed, my sister is the new queen, I fell in love with someone who might be dead and who definitely has another secret queen on his hook, and oh, by the way, I hope you've been well since I sent you away after leading you on for the last two years.*

But she didn't have to say all that, because a guard burst through the trees and threw himself at Alaric. Ros yelled, or she thought she did, because her voice was suddenly raw. If she did, Alaric showed no sign he'd noticed. He drew his own sword, parried the guard's blows, and put his blade straight through the man's neck.

Alaric stood there a moment, sword poised for another attack, but none came. After a moment, he turned back to Ros and said, "Right then. Let's get out of here."

She trailed behind him for half an hour without further indication they were being followed before she finally asked, "Where are we going?"

"The rendezvous point, of course."

"How do you know about that?"

"Because I picked it."

"You picked the super-secret meeting place for the rebel band of loyalists?"

"Rosa, who do you think started the Tide?"

She opened her mouth to answer, closed it again. She hadn't considered it before now. In her mind, it had been something to do with her little sister, not her former lover. "I thought Elsa..."

"She made it legitimate, I'll give her that. We were nameless and basically leaderless before she came into the picture."

Ros bit her lip, unsure about the words banging

through her head. But she had to say them, to see if there was truth in them. "I think she betrayed me."

Alaric stopped walking and turned to face her. "Hear this now and never forget it: your sister has never and will never betray you. She loves you bone-deep. I don't know what she did that makes you think she betrayed you, but I am certain she did it to save you, not hurt you."

And just like that, her fears dissipated. Once she heard Alaric's proclamation, she knew it was true. Elsa must've known something Ros didn't and she made plans to get Ros out of the castle and moved to safety, because that was the only way she could keep her safe.

"You're right," Ros said. "I know you're right."

"Good, then onward we go."

"Where is this rendezvous point, anyway?"

Alaric winced. "You're not going to like it."

"Is that why no one would tell me?"

"Probably," he laughed.

"After everything else that's happened, I think I can handle it."

He nodded. "Right, then. In two days, we'll meet the rest of the Rising Tide at Earth house."

Eight

Ros was certain she had misheard him. There was no way they were going to Earth house. With both her mother and the Zoltos pushing her off the throne, it was the home of nearly *all* her enemies.

Well, maybe that was a stretch. Enemies seemed to come from everywhere all at once, with Hessian Barclay of Air and Gaius Scalise of Night among them. Fire house was the only one that hadn't betrayed her yet, and with the way things were going, it was only a matter of time.

Still though, Earth house?

"I'm sorry," Ros said as they trudged along, "but I need some clarification if you said what I think you said."

Alaric said, "Think about it. It's the last place they would look."

"Because I'd have to be a fool to go there."

"And you're no fool."

She stared open-mouthed at him, her brow bent in confusion as she attempted to follow his thought process. "But if I would have to be a fool to go there, and I'm going there, doesn't that absolutely make me the fool I'm trying not to be?"

"Not in the least," he said, pushing aside a large branch that blocked their path. "You know it would be foolish to go there and that they won't expect it, but you are taking a calculated risk in going anyway. If anything, you are weighing your options with competence and bravery, and choosing the least expected path."

"Technically, I'm not choosing anything. *You* chose the rendezvous point."

He shrugged. "No one has ever accused me of being anything *but* a fool."

"You're not inspiring a great deal of confidence in this decision."

"Good thing I only have to be a rebel leader until your throne is secure. Then I can go back to just being a quality blacksmith with a work contract with the royal family in perpetuity."

Ros chuckled. "That explains it."

"Explains what?"

"Your motivation. I've been wondering why you were doing this. An unending agreement to outfit the castle's needs is quite the reward."

Alaric stopped walking, but didn't turn to her. "That's not why I'm doing this."

"But you just said—"

"Aye, I know what I said. That's the deal your sister offered me *after* I'd already started gathering people to our cause. It's an excellent motivator, sure, but it isn't the reason I'm here."

"Then why?"

She could hear the rush of her heart in her ears as they stood in silence for two, three, four heartbeats. Finally, he said, "Do you really have to ask?"

When she didn't answer, Alaric started through the trees again, Ros trailing behind him. He was right. Ros knew exactly why he was helping her and it was cruel of her to accept his sacrifice when she couldn't return the feelings he had for her. He had made his declaration of love in her bedroom the night the Elementalists had come for the Great Match and she had refused him. She would always have to refuse him. There was no chance for love between the two of them, no matter what either of them felt.

There was no doubt that if her life had been different, she could've loved Alaric. If he was a noble or she was a villager, if there wasn't so much in the way between mages and magicless, if a dozen other things had aligned differently...

But they hadn't. She had been born into the royal family. Even if she could change it, she wouldn't—not for Alaric or anyone else—because by luck or fate or something else entirely, she had the chance to serve Talabrih and make it better. If she could get her throne back, anyway. And though she never wanted to be queen for power's sake, she *did* want to take care of the Talabrisians who needed her. Just because she'd never had a choice in the matter didn't mean she wasn't perfect for the role.

If she couldn't get the throne back, she wasn't sure what would become of her, but she did know that as enjoyable as it had been, her time with Alaric had already passed. He was kind, handsome, generous, and would make a wonderful husband for some lucky girl, but it wouldn't be her.

Even if everything else miraculously aligned, she'd followed through with the plan for her life and chosen a mage from the Great Match. To everyone in the kingdom, the mage she'd chosen was Lyzandor Zolto. But in truth, Rosalinde's heart now belonged to Cassian Scalise. She wasn't sure how yet, but she would find her way back to him. In her heart, she knew they were inevitable.

THEY REACHED the village of Chambron just before dawn. It was a midway point on the way to Earth house and hopefully a place to find shelter during the day. They hadn't run into any guards after Alaric killed the one chasing her, but they expected to see them on the roads at first light. By now Water house would have organized their sizable forces and started the hunt. Hopefully, Chambron would be a place of refuge, even if only for a few hours after the exhausting night.

They stayed hidden at the forest's edge, skirting along the perimeter of the town, though for the most part the place looked as if it was still asleep. Alaric assured her the nearby farmers would already be awake and working, but the merchants in town seemed to rise a little later.

At the southern edge of Chambron, Alaric put his left hand on the hilt of his sword and took Rosalinde's hand with his right as he whispered, "Stay close and keep your head down."

He led her out of the forest's shadow and crept along the side of a building that was slightly set apart from the others. He peered around the corner for an eternity before finally dragging Ros out of the building's shadow and around to the front door.

Alaric tapped out a strange knock that almost sounded like a heartbeat. A moment later, there was rustling inside and the door opened. Inside was dark and Ros couldn't see anything about the place or the person who had opened the door.

She asked, "Where are—"

"Shhh," a voice hissed.

She turned her head back and forth, searching for the voice, but could see naught in the heavy darkness. Alaric squeezed her hand, as if to reassure her it was okay to follow the stranger she couldn't see, and he pulled her along through the building. She only stumbled twice and would have been proud of herself except for how sure-footed Alaric seemed despite the darkness.

She wondered if he'd always been like this. Aside

from sneaking across the castle grounds for a handsy make-out session, she'd never gone anywhere with him. How could she? She couldn't be openly seen with a commoner, for his sake as much as hers. She had no doubt the nobles would have made both their lives hell if they'd known of their relationship, and she'd not wanted to put him through that for something that had a set expiration date anyway. Her world was too cruel for someone as kind-hearted as Alaric.

Still, as he led her through the room with such effort-less grace, she wondered what other things she didn't know about him. Everyone she thought she knew seemed to be full of secrets these days.

There was a creaking sound ahead of them and Ros saw the outline of a door with warm light burning behind it. They stepped through the door and into the room, the door closing behind them. Ros turned to see a child scurry from pushing the door closed to hide behind their father's leg. Rosalinde smiled as the little face peeked around to sneak a glimpse of her.

The room itself wasn't large and a forge in the back of the room took up most of it. There were piles of metal, a wrack with weapons, and an anvil behind the father and child. They must've walked through the front of the smithy, or maybe even a storefront, to get to this more private workroom.

"Where are the others?" the man asked.

The question hit Ros, sending her gut plummeting like a stone thrown into a lake. Part of her wanted to cower away, knowing she was the reason they were missing; another part wanted to tell how they begged and pleaded for Ros to run away, to save herself, but she knew it wouldn't absolve her of the guilt she felt. She did what they told her to do and felt terrible about it. Even worse, she hadn't thought of them in longer than she cared to admit. Fleeing through the night at Alaric's side, her thoughts had been so full of finding safety that she'd blocked out nearly everything else, including her friends' sacrifices.

She opened her mouth to speak, but found no words waiting on her tongue. There was nothing she could say to make sense of the last day.

"They're meeting us elsewhere," Alaric said.

Ros noticed the tightness in his tone, the careful answer that didn't actually answer anything. Alaric didn't fully trust this man.

"I was told—"

"Things change, Saul. Rebellions aren't precise."

Rebellions, Ros thought. The word suddenly had so much gravitas. Alaric had called himself a rebel leader, but Ros hadn't taken him seriously. In the woods, despite everything, he had seemed like the carefree boy she'd known these last couple of years; now though, she looked at him with fresh eyes.

Something was *changed* in him. He seemed to have a rigidity to his demeanor, an assertive confidence that she'd never seen. Alaric had always seemed so go-lucky and accommodating, unwilling to decide when someone else could do it instead. That was part of why the confession of his feelings had felt so out of place—someone else had already decided it and his input changed nothing. Maybe this side of him had always been there, and she just hadn't noticed. Perhaps she'd only seen what she wanted to, so that he'd fill the role she'd assigned him and wouldn't endanger either of their hearts by being something more.

"So the actual members of our party didn't make it, but you brought *her* here?"

"She's with us."

"That's inconvenient. Hard to rebel against the throne when you're carting a royal across the kingdom," Saul said. "Expect it will be hard to keep the rebels alive, too, since the enemy has been invited into my safe-house and seen my face."

"She's the reason we're doing this in the first place," Alaric said.

"Nah, she's the reason *you're* doing it. The rest of us understand that she's just the latest in a long line of oppressors." Saul's hand slid to the hilt at his waist. "The only good royal is a dead one."

Alaric took two strides across the room until he was nose-to-nose with Saul. "She is under my protection. Brother or not, I wouldn't recommend you challenge me in this."

Brother? Why hadn't he ever told her of a brother?

"Grow up, Ric," Saul said. "Use your head instead of your dick."

Alaric growled, "This isn't about *that*."

"Of course it is. You wouldn't be doing this for someone else. I guarantee she knows it, and is using your affection to keep her throne," Saul said, waving a hand at Ros.

She started to protest, but Alaric spoke over whatever she was going to say. "We are not rebelling against the throne. We're trying to change a corrupt system. It isn't going to happen overnight. We *need* someone on the throne who will fight for us."

"You think it's going to be her?"

"I do," Alaric said. He glanced over his shoulder, the hard lines of his face softening when his eyes met hers. "She's not like the others."

Saul scoffed and stepped past Alaric toward Ros. "They're all the same. The best thing we could do is get rid of the system altogether. If that's not an option, we remove her and put one of our own in her place."

"The nobles would never allow it," Ros said, finally finding her voice. Though the words were her first impulse, she immediately knew it was the wrong thing to say.

Saul's eyes narrowed at her. "They won't be able to object if all their throats are cut."

Ros smirked, relishing the look on Saul's face when his violent comment didn't spook her. She lifted her hand to eye level as magic danced across her fingertips. "Easier said than done. The nobles could crush a rebellion with a third of the force, because they have the power."

"You've worked to keep it that way, too," Saul said.

"It's not our fault that the magic stays with the nobles," Ros said, though the words tasted sour as she said them.

Saul put his hands on his hips and tipped his head back in a laugh. "Oh, right. That's definitely not the reason for the marriage restrictions. Noble blood marries noble blood, or as your ancestors figured out ages ago, magic blood doesn't tarnish itself with the magicless."

"Obviously we want to preserve the strength of magic—" she began.

"Because that's what keeps you in power," Saul interrupted.

She wanted to rebut his argument, but couldn't. Not if she was being honest with herself. She'd always questioned the marriage rules among the nobility, but it was never something she could fix. Ros was as encumbered by the laws as everyone else, her future planned from the time she was a child. What would her life have looked like without such things?

"That's not entirely true," she said, but she felt the weakness in her words. Maybe it *wasn't* entirely true, but there was enough truth in it to jar her thinking.

The door behind them creaked, and everyone turned to the woman who entered. She was lovely, with gentle features and a pillow-soft body. Her hair was pulled back, but thin pieces had slipped loose and formed a halo around her face.

"Am I interrupting?" she asked, her lips puckering into a heart.

"Not at all, Clarissa." Alaric smiled and moved across the room, pulling her into an embrace. "It's good to see you."

She said, "It's been too long. But at least this time you brought a girl with you."

"Right," Alaric said. He motioned to the woman and said, "Clarie, this is Queen Rosalinde Managold."

Clarie swatted Alaric's arm and said, "I know who she is."

"Pleasure to meet you," Ros said, dipping into a curtsy. "Call me Ros."

The woman's mouth spread into a wide grin and she grabbed Alaric's arm, whispering, "Ricky, she just bowed to me."

"She can hear you, Clarie," he stage-whispered back.

"Of course," she said, her smile still beaming.

Saul sighed and crossed his arms over his chest. "Are you really fawning over her when you know what she stands for?"

Clarie's eyes bulged as she said, "Honey, you know I support you and the rebellion, but what do you expect when there's a princess in the forge?"

"Queen," Alaric corrected.

"Oh, right, I'm so sorry."

"It's fine," Ros said.

Clarie stepped toward her and wrapped her arms around Ros, saying, "I'm so, so sorry. You poor thing."

Ros realized the woman wasn't apologizing for using the wrong title. She was sharing her condolences about the disappearance of her father. Without knowledge of what had really happened, it would make sense that the magicless thought he was dead.

"Come on, let's get some tea," Clarie said. She put her hand on Rosalinde's back and led her out of the forge. Calling back over her shoulder, she said, "Breakfast in twenty. There'd better not be any blood on your faces when you get there."

Nine

Clarie led Ros back through the dim hall to the front room where they'd first entered the building. The shutters were still closed, so Ros couldn't see the light outside, but at least Clarie had lit a lamp so they could see to walk through the room.

As Ros had guessed, they used the front as a store for the things Saul created. Though she'd noticed plenty of weapons around the forge, most of what she saw in the front room was farming tools, nails, and basic household items. She supposed it made sense. While Alaric crafted weaponry for nobles and those in the city around the castle, his brother catered to a smaller area and would serve a different clientele.

Clarie took Ros up a side staircase and into a small living area. She offered her a seat, and though initially Ros intended to stay on her feet, the mere thought of sitting made her realize how bone-tired she was. She plopped down in the chair while Clarie set about making breakfast.

A tug at her hair jerked Ros awake. She hadn't realized she'd been dozing, but the weight of all that had happened was clearly taking its toll on her.

"You have such pretty hair," a small voice said.

Ros glanced over her shoulder to see the small face of the child who had been hiding behind Saul's legs. The girl was stick-thin, pale like her mother, with hair that could pass for straw. Ros forced a smile onto her tired face and said, "Thank you."

"It's a shame, really."

"What's a shame, Winnie?" Clarie asked, turning from her preparations.

"That daddy hates her so much. I did this for him," the girl said as she walked around the table holding a clump of Rosalinde's hair. In a sing-song voice she said, "Cut your hair, cut your throat, see if lying queens can float..."

Clarie's hand shot to her mouth. "Oh child, what have you done?" She fell onto the kitchen floor at Rosalinde's feet and said, "Please, milady, punish me in her stead. She's too young to know better. It's my fault for not teaching her right."

Ros looked from the mass of hair in the girl's hand to her dirty, grinning face, then down at her horrified mother. She reached her hand around and felt the uneven hair at the back of her head. Suddenly, without warning, Ros began to laugh.

It was a strange sound even to herself; her laugh was the chaotic high-pitched tone of someone who'd gone out for the day and left their brain at home. It hit all at once—the deep ache of missing her father, the hurt of her mother's betrayal, the fear and grief of losing her throne and her home in one fell swoop, the loss of her companionship with Alaric, the confusion about her relationship with Cassian or if they even still had one. It was too much.

"It's just hair," she heard someone say, two, three, four times.

Then she realized it was her voice. And she was right, of course. It was just hair, and it didn't really matter. Except it wasn't just hair. It was heartache and guilt and bitterness and regret and a hundred other things that the child seemed to hold in her small hand. That clump of hair was yet another thing out of Rosalinde's control, another thing that had changed that she couldn't fix.

Ros felt warm, powerful hands lift her up and found herself looking into Alaric's kind eyes. She sighed and let her head fall against his chest as he carried her away from the table. A moment later, he released her onto a bed. She felt his arms pulling away, but she grabbed him and pulled him down into the bed with her. She needed his warmth beside her—the security only felt when someone who cared for you was near.

It was cruel, and she knew it, but Ros refused to think about it right then. In only a few weeks, her entire world had crashed around her and Alaric was the only thing left of who she was before the explosion. Things had irrevocably changed between them, but he was still here, and that was enough for this moment.

She rolled onto her side and he tucked in behind her, the shape of him as familiar as her own skin. Ros could feel Alaric's breath tickle her ear and neck as he combed the leftover pieces of her hair out of the way.

"It doesn't look that bad," he whispered.

Ros laughed, but this time it wasn't the manic laughter of someone losing themselves; no, it was a comfortable thing between friends, an easiness from letting down her guard—it was a refuge.

"I'll start a new trend," Ros whispered.

His body shook against her back as he laughed. "Probably not, but it's fixable."

"I'll just look ridiculous in the meantime."

"Not to me," he said, his voice serious, but soft. "To me, you are perfect."

It was the last thing Ros heard as she drifted into a heavy, dreamless, contented sleep.

Ros woke when the blade poked into her neck. She jerked back and threw her hands up, magic springing to her fingers. She loosed a tsunami against her assailant, sending a wave of water across the room and slamming them into the wall. As the water dissipated, Ros stood to counter a further attack, but it didn't come.

Then she saw the small, pale body with straw blonde hair lying motionless on the floor.

"Is everything okay?" Clarie asked as she rushed through the door.

She looked from Ros, her hands still held up with magic sparking along her fingertips, to the prone body of her daughter. She dived to the floor by the child, screaming her name over and over, though the girl didn't utter a sound.

"What's going on?" Alaric asked as he entered the room. He put his hands on Rosalinde's shoulders, forcing her panicked eyes to focus on him. In an even tone, he said, "Tell me what happened."

"Sh-she had a knife to my throat," Ros sputtered. "Woke me up. I just reacted. I didn't know."

"You need to calm down," he said, pushing her down on the bed.

He took her hands in his, his eyes still locked on hers. Each time she tried to look at the child, Alaric forced her gaze back to his. The moment stretched on and felt as if a great deal of time had passed, but as Ros eased herself and her magic back from the edge, she realized it must've only been a few seconds. Clarie was still screaming her daughter's name.

"I'm okay," Ros said.

Alaric looked down at her hands, and she realized he was checking for a sign of magic. When he saw none, he met her eyes and gave a quick nod before moving to the floor to check on Winnie. Ros watched from the bed, afraid to move closer, as Alaric performed compressions on her chest.

Time passed in a slow arc around them, never touching the moment that trapped them. Alaric stopped and slumped to the side with a terse shake of his head. Clarie wailed even louder than before.

Ros heard boots on the steps, and Saul ran into the room. He saw his daughter on the floor soaking wet, then his hardened face turned on Ros. "You did this."

"No," Clarie said, rising to her feet. There was no softness left in her, only the venom of someone with nothing left to lose. "*You* did this with your anger at the nobles and your talk of rising against them."

"What are you talking about?"

"She attacked the queen in her sleep. Jabbed a knife against her throat," Clarie yelled.

"That means nothing. She could've been playing."

Clarie spat, "She did this to make you proud."

She shoved her hands against her husband's chest. Though she couldn't have pushed the hulking man that hard, he jumped away from her in terror. Smoke issued up from two hand-shaped burn marks on his shirt.

Saul's eyes turned from surprise to disgust. "You're one of *them*."

For her part, Clarie looked just as surprised as he had. She stared down at her hands, confusion and fear battling for priority on her face.

"We don't have time for this," Ros said, finally

finding her voice amidst the chaos. "We need to get her to a Healer."

"For what?" Saul spat. "We can't pay. All our money's tied to this failing rebellion."

Ros was aghast. "Pay? The village Healer should perform their duties for free."

"We don't live in your fairytale world, *Highness.*"

She clenched her jaws and ground out, "Fine. I'll do it myself."

She strode across the room. No one else knew she had access to multiple magics, but it couldn't stay secret forever. Not if she was going to right this wrong.

Before she'd made it to Winnie, Saul grabbed her arm and swung her back toward him. "You are no Healer and your magic has done enough. Let my girl rest in peace."

"I can save her," Ros said, trying to pull her arm free.

"Maybe if your father was here," Saul said. "He was a terrible king, like all those before him, but at least he had magic that was useful."

Ros looked over her shoulder to where Alaric still sat on the floor by Winnie. He was lost there, unseeing the rest of what had unfolded. She called out, "Alaric, please."

He looked up, blinking away a daze. "What are you doing?"

"I can help her," Ros said. "You have to trust me."

"You're not going near her body," Saul said, squeezing Rosalinde's arm painfully.

"Let her go," Alaric said, climbing to his feet.

He crossed the room in a flash, barreling into Saul. Alaric's motion caught Saul by surprise, and his grip on Ros loosened just enough for her to jerk her arm free.

Ros slid to the floor beside Winnie while the men tumbled into the next room. The child's lips were blue, her skin as pale as snow. Ros realized then what Alaric had been trying to do; Rosalinde's tsunami had drowned the child and he was trying to push the air back into her lungs.

She put her hands on the girl's chest and thought about water, the easy way it sprang up when she needed it. This time, however, she reached for the water still in Winnie, calling it back to herself. Ros focused on each drop as it trickled out of the child's nose and bubbled out of her mouth.

Ros felt the completeness of her magic when the last of the water returned to her. It wasn't something she'd noticed before, but now she knew without a doubt that every molecule of water that had exited her fingers had now returned.

She didn't know how to heal someone like her father or Teague did, so instead she turned her attention to air. Ros focused on her own breath going in and out of her body. It only took a few seconds to attune herself to the way the air felt as it flowed into her lungs, but she still had to figure out how to get it to do that for someone else.

Ros kneeled over Winnie and opened her mouth. She pushed the air out of her own body and into the girl's, willing it to use the memory of her lungs inside the young child. The air left her body, ignoring Rosalinde's pleas.

She did it again, willing her breath into the girl. Again, it didn't work.

Ros knew they were out of time. Though everything had felt like slow motion, it had only taken a minute to play out. Still, that was too long for someone to go without breathing.

One last try, she thought.

She closed her eyes and let her magic consume her, burn through her. Ros let herself *become* the magic. When she leaned forward and breathed air into Winnie, she went with it. She traveled through the child's body, teaching the air she moved with how to expand and contract within the lungs.

In, out.

In, out.

She moved through the girl's lungs with each forced breath, filling and refilling every part of the expanse, until she felt the magic that was in her, that *was* her, understand. Once she knew the air would stay and keep working, she let her consciousness travel back outside and return to herself.

There was a terrible racking cough that echoed through the room as Ros opened her eyes. Winnie's cough was violent, distressing, but her body was taking in air, pushing it back out, over and over on its own.

That hideous cough was the most beautiful sound Ros had ever heard.

ROS AND ALARIC left as soon as they knew Winnie was okay. It was early evening and there was more light outside than either would have liked, but they didn't have a choice. The fight between Alaric and Saul didn't end when Winnie started breathing again, and might not have ended if Clarie hadn't stepped forward and set the rug they were rolling on ablaze. It was a small fire, the size a child might set when they first found their magic, but it stopped the tussle, nonetheless.

Ros wasn't sure what to make of Clarie's fire magic. She'd never heard of a commoner having magic or suddenly developing powers under duress. Then again, she was discovering a lot of strange, true things lately that were myths or old stories come to life. The scary part was that Clarie had these powers and had no idea how to use them or who to teach her. If Ros tried to get her help, the poor woman could end up in the dungeon simply for existing outside the nobles' rules. If she didn't get help for her, she could hurt someone. There was no way to know which path to take.

Ultimately, she decided there wasn't anything to be done right now. She warned Clarie not to use her powers if she didn't have to and explained the most basic things she knew about using fire magic. Her time stealing library books since the coronation had done some good, at least, giving her a framework for Clarie to build on.

After their talk about magic, Ros had hugged Clarie and begged her forgiveness for hurting Winnie. The woman had pulled back and looked Ros in her eyes with a hardness that hadn't been there that morning. "It was an accident and we all know it, even if I'm the only one who will say it. Saul's the one who should apologize for what he's done to my girl. But don't you fret about it, My Queen, I'll set her right. I may be a rebel against the system, but I believe in you."

As she and Alaric turned to leave, Clarie called out for them to stop. She gave Ros a tattered dress and cloak to get her out of the lounging gown she was still wearing, then turned Ros around and sheared off the rest of her hair. There was no mirror for Ros to check her reflection, but as they walked away from the forge and Rosalinde's once long hair now bounced along her shoulders with each step, she knew she had to look a mess.

Then she caught sight of Alaric staring at her with the purest look of love she'd ever seen. She blushed at his gaze, and suddenly her new haircut didn't feel nearly as terrible.

They'd left the town quickly and headed for the cover of the woods. This part of the kingdom seemed perpetually green, a blanket of forests that camouflaged the land.

After they were far enough away from town, Alaric

asked, "Are we going to talk about how you healed someone with magic you shouldn't have access to?"

"Wasn't planning on it."

Alaric nodded and didn't press. That was something Ros loved about him—he didn't need to understand the details to trust her.

"Anything else we need to talk about?"

Ros chewed her lip for a moment before whispering, "No."

She knew it was the wrong answer, but it was the only one she had for him right then. They trekked in silence; Ros knew they *needed* the quiet, especially while there was still daylight, but in the back of her head she couldn't help but wonder if the silence between them was somehow more than that.

She knew she couldn't avoid thinking about those few minutes of comfort lying in Alaric's arms. Eventually, they'd have to talk about it. She owed him that, probably an apology as well, though she couldn't seem to make all of herself feel truly sorry. There were a lot of things they needed to talk about, if Ros was being honest. She wasn't happy with the way they'd left things before the Great Match, but no matter how many times she replayed it in her head, she wasn't sure what else she could have done.

Alaric deserved a better life than the secret lover role she could offer him, if she could even offer him that. She wasn't sure where things stood in her life right now. Dragging him along into her chaos was selfish. Despite knowing this to her core, those few minutes in his arms had felt like going home. Though she'd developed feelings for Cassian in their short time together, her relationship with Alaric had bloomed over time and grown deeper than what she'd been able to forge with Cassian thus far. She couldn't deny there was still something joining them together, even after she'd tried to pull them apart.

Ros jolted out of her thoughts as Alaric stopped in front of her. She whispered, "What's wrong?"

"Put your hood up," he said. Alaric kneeled and scooped up a handful of dirt. He smeared his thumb across Rosalinde's cheek and streaked a bit down his own before tossing the rest at the bottom of her dress. "That's better."

Ros swatted at the dirt storm, trying to hide how much the grime bothered her. "In what world is that *better*?"

"In the world we're living in, Rosa," he said. "With your hair cut, an old dress, and some dirt on you, we can get out of these woods and follow the road without attracting attention."

"Are you sure that's safe?"

"Nothing we do is safe. But two weary travelers on the side of the road are a lot less suspicious than people creeping through the forest. With evening coming on, most people won't pay a dirty peasant girl a second glance."

She bit her lip, weighing his words. "It seems like an

unnecessary risk. But you know more about this sort of thing than I do, so I'll trust your judgment."

Alaric laughed as he led her out of the shadow of the trees and toward the road. "Yeah, I traipse around the kingdom with dethroned monarchs *all* the time."

"You might," she said. "For all I know, you've led a hundred rebellions and you've got a queen in every kingdom."

"I can see why you would think that. In addition to being very good at rebelling, I'm also incredibly handsome. Most queens do have trouble resisting me."

"I can imagine," she said. "It's a miracle I'm able to keep my dress on in your presence."

"There was a time when you couldn't."

Though he was teasing, Rosalinde's cheeks flushed, and she recognized the truth in his words. "We're all guilty of doing foolish things in our youth."

"Ah yes, the brainless acts of adolescence. I'm so grateful you've found such wisdom now that you're a month older."

Despite Alaric's jovial tone, she could sense the bitterness in him. There was no longer any chance of putting off the conversation. Honestly, she had put it off too long already. She sighed and asked, "What do you want me to say? I know things ended badly between us, definitely not the way I wanted them to, but what other choice did I have?"

"Why did things have to end at all?"

The question caught her off guard. It wasn't just the

words he spoke, but the sincere confusion he seemed to have. They had always known it would end this way... or at least Ros had always known. She thought it was a mutual understanding, since neither of them had ever broached the subject. It wasn't as if the Great Match was a new concept; nobles had been using it for decades to determine their marriages. As far as Ros was concerned, it had always seemed like the natural end to their relationship.

When things were new and exciting, there was no need to think about the future; they had their stolen moments and made good use of them. Those fleeting minutes seemed like they would last forever. As things had gotten more serious between them and they'd started sharing more than just their bodies, Ros had thought they didn't talk about the end because it was pointless. Now she realized their outlooks on things had been far more different than she could have imagined. Had Alaric truly never considered what would happen when she reached the age of marriage?

Rosalinde's voice was soft when she asked something she'd never thought to ask before: "What did you think would happen when it was time for me to marry?"

"I don't know," he said, kicking a rock off the road. "I guess I just thought you'd fall madly in love with me, defy your parents and generations of tradition, and we'd run away together as dirty, happy peasants."

He smiled over at her as if he were joking, but Ros saw right through it. Alaric might try to play his words off, but they were real. He had really expected her to abandon her family, her responsibilities, her kingdom for him.

And, she thought, *maybe I should have.*

But those words didn't come out, sticking in her throat and sinking back down to be buried in her heart once more. What good would it do to say such things?

Instead, she said, "I care for you, of course. If things were different…"

The sound of an approaching wagon stopped her from finishing her sentence. Oh, that blessed traveler that kept her from uttering words that condemned her fickle heart! This time with Alaric reminded her of how deeply she adored him, how much she had *loved* him, despite the heartache she knew that love would beget. Throughout their time together, she'd never uttered those words to him. She certainly shouldn't today.

Besides, her heart was someone else's now, wasn't it? She'd felt a kinship with Cassian, drawing her ever closer even when she'd wanted to step away. And though she hadn't chosen him because of circumstances beyond her control, she still had hope that his feelings remained and they would figure out a way to make things work. At least with Cassian there was a chance, since he was noble —it was more than Alaric had ever had.

The wagon slowed to a stop beside them. Alaric grabbed Ros by the hand and pulled her body behind his in a way that was quite conspicuous. He looked up at the wagon driver and said, "Good evening, friend."

"Aye, so it is, so far at least," the driver said. She was an older woman, mid-sixties or so, with short white hair shorn close to her head. Her brows were still dark, once black, but now faded to charcoal, and knit together over shockingly blue eyes.

"Might you be headed to Earth house?" Alaric asked.

The woman frowned. "Not sure how that's your business, son."

"Forgive my husband," Ros said, stepping out from behind him. "We're travel-worn and weary, but it's no excuse for a lack of manners. That we'll blame on his mother."

The woman's lips curled at the corner. "Plenty of mothers forget the necessity of manners when their babe is a boy, as if being a man is blessing enough. They let them learn what they want and foul up the rest. Instead, it's women who are held to a higher standard, aye, lass?"

Ros nodded agreeably, adding, "We're aiming for Earth house, hoping to put our hands to work. Any chance you have room for a polite young woman and a foolish man in need of a good scolding?"

This time, the woman's mouth went into a full grin. "I can make some room if you'll allow me the privilege of rebuking him for the next few hours."

"It would be my pleasure," Ros said. "Maybe he'll listen to you since he sure won't listen to anything I tell him."

"You dismiss the wisdom of your wife?" she asked,

not even letting them get aboard before she started her lecture.

And so they continued through the evening and well into the night, listening to the gravelly voice of Aggy, for that was her name, as she harangued Alaric for a thousand and one crimes against the wife who would never be his.

Ten

T he morning light shone bright against Rosalinde's eyelids, waking her from a bumpy sleep in the back of Aggy's wagon. She lay there with her eyes closed for a few minutes, pretending she was anywhere but there.

"I know you're awake," Aggy said, a smile coloring her voice.

Ros opened her eyes. The sky above wasn't sunny as she'd expected, but overcast and glaringly white. Ros winced at the light and rolled over to stare at the rolling forests instead. Only there weren't any rolling forests. Fields of vibrant hues colored the land on either side of the road in perfect geometric designs of squares, triangles, octagons, decagons, and some shapes unfamiliar to her.

"Where are we?"

"'Bout an hour south of Earth house proper."

"An hour? I didn't think we'd get there until later afternoon."

"Made good time while you were getting your beauty rest," Aggy said.

Ros pulled her hood up to shield her eyes as she stared in silence at the gardens they passed. It made sense that this road led to the home of the great Botanical mages of Earth house, but something about it bothered Ros. She clambered up to sit in the front of Aggy's cart. "It wasn't like this the last time I came through."

"Been a few years since you've been up this way?" Aggy asked. Not waiting for an answer, she continued, "The house nobles decided to make this 'more attractive' to encourage visitors. They didn't want their poor folk to be as visible."

"Yeah," Ros said slowly, remembering the way the land looked the last time she visited. "I haven't been through Earth house for years. Last time I was here, there were small fields of crops haphazardly crawling together with houses dotting the land here and there. You could see forest far behind it all, but they always seemed so far away that it would take ages to reach them, if you ever did. And behind it all was a sky that never dulled."

"That's a romantic memory for a place that both birthed and killed the people who lived here, one after another, never able to leave the hand dealt to them. Or maybe just a kind way of calling the place an eyesore. Guess that's what I get for insisting on manners."

Ros hadn't seen it that way. She'd watched children

running down the road alongside the royal caravan, happier than any noble child she'd ever seen. There were wildflowers along the road back then, and a bramble of berry bushes picked clean by purple-stained hands. It had been years since she visited Earth house, but she still remembered the way it filled her with a sweet melancholy she'd never known before. This new design was beautiful, but it was strategic and precise—two words that should never be used to describe growing things.

"I don't imagine you appreciate this place for what it is," Aggy said. "This land was a beggar's cemetery. When you're too poor to live anywhere else, you get tossed out here to beg travelers for money. You might get lucky and find somebody else in the same shape as you, build a home around that mutual misery, but what you saw when you visited and what it really was are vastly different things."

Ros breathed, "I had no idea."

"Course not. No one's gonna show that if they don't have to. The house lords cleaned it up from time to time, especially when they knew high folks were coming. Then when the new Lady of Earth house took her place, she cleaned it up for good."

"What happened to all the people who lived here?"

"Moved on to better lands, places where they ain't seen. I know it seems cruel to hide the lower parts of society from you outsiders and try to make our lands seem more than what they are, but you don't know what it's like to come from a house that's spent decades

sending our wealth out to other houses instead of distrib-
uting it within. Everybody wants to visit Water house
and see the king in his grand castle, while the other
houses are forgotten. It's our turn, see; time to stop
forgetting us."

Ros glanced at the old woman. Her tone had
remained the same, but her words were harsher and her
hands gripped the cart reins so hard that her knuckles
were white. Ros looked around, suddenly realizing she'd
been so caught up in the countryside that she hadn't realized Alaric was nowhere to be seen.

"Aggy," Ros asked, her voice as steady as she could
make it. "Where's my husband?"

The old woman laughed, a terrible, vicious sound.
"Your husband, that *is* rich. You're supposed to be
marrying a good Earth house boy and helping us gain the
prosperity we deserve, not slumming it with some magicless buffoon."

Ros went rigid, realizing the awful mistake they'd
made by coming out of the shelter of the forest. A bad
haircut and dirty dress would never be enough to hide
one of the most famous faces in the land.

"There's clearly been a mistake," Ros started, letting
magic trickle to her fingertips.

Thick vines shot up from the cart seat, wrapping
themselves around Rosalinde's legs and wrists. Ros
jerked one hand free and let loose a firebolt at one of the
vines, but three more slithered up and took its place.
They pulled her hands apart, binding them down onto

the seat on either side of her body and wrapping so tightly around them they looked like they were part of the wooden bench on which she sat.

"Sit there and mind your impeccable, lady-like manners," Aggy said. "It doesn't have to get any worse. We can still enjoy a civil conversation on the last leg of the trip."

"Start by telling me what you've done to Alaric."

"*Start by telling what you've done to Alaric,*" Aggy mocked, rolling her eyes. "Start by telling me how a Water mage just used a firebolt."

They both sat in silence for several minutes, neither giving ground. Finally, Aggy said, "You ever heard of asking nicely? I thought we'd been over this. Saying please goes a long way."

Ros clenched her jaws together, grinding out the words: "Please. Tell. Me. Where. He. Is."

"Was that so hard?" Aggy asked. They bobbed along the road for another minute before Aggy finally said, "I didn't kill him, if that's what you're thinking. He's tied to a tree a ways back. Won't be getting free anytime soon."

But he's alive, Ros thought, letting the relief flood over her. She sighed, asking, "What are you going to do with me?"

Aggy puckered her lips in thought, her brows creasing. "Not sure. There's a big reward if I take you back to your sister, and since I'm headed back that way tomorrow, the thought has crossed my mind."

"You know they'll kill me if you take me back."

Aggy nodded. "The guards spreading the word around your castle said dead or alive. Sounds like you pissed 'em off something fierce."

"I was protecting an Earth house boy," Ros said. "Or at least that's what elevated my trouble. I imagine they were already looking for a way to oust me before that."

"What boy?"

"Beckett Chastain."

Aggy sat in silence for a moment before finally muttering, "So you're the reason they didn't ship him home? His father's been sore about him lingering at Water house."

Ros wasn't sure what answer the woman was looking for, but at this point it didn't matter either way. She was already a prisoner. "I promised I would keep him safe, let him make his own decisions about coming home. I did everything I could to keep that promise."

Aggy's pursed mouth moved in a circle, as if she was chewing Rosalinde's words. "I've known that boy his whole life. He's a good kid, dealt a bad hand. It means a lot that you'd help him."

Ros added up what she knew about Aggy. She had Earth magic and was clearly a noblewoman, even if she tried to hide it. Her mannerisms and the way she carried herself gave her away. She likely wasn't rich, or she wouldn't be pulling a wagon back and forth between houses. If she'd known Beckett his whole life, it wasn't as a servant. A relative, maybe?

"How are you related to him?"

"Smarter than you look, I'll give you that," Aggy said. "Beckett is my wife's nephew. We haven't been allowed to see him since he started having 'tendencies,' as his pissant father likes to call them."

"Why does he have such a problem with who a person loves? It doesn't affect him."

"No, it doesn't, but he holds a grudge. You see, Beckett's father was in love once, with a lovely young girl who didn't know herself very well yet. And this girl was brought to live in their very fine home to be groomed to be Andrew's bride. The family was kind and welcoming, and the girl grew especially close to Andrew's sister. So close, in fact, that the two fell madly in love and ran away together. Andrew did not take it well, as he was raised in a way that made it clear that he could have whoever and whatever he wanted, whenever. He considered that young girl his property, not his equal. Though he loved her in his own way, it wasn't the genuine sort of love she found elsewhere. He's held it against every gay person he's met since."

"So that's how you became his aunt instead of his mother."

Aggy nodded. "Andrew forgave his sister in time, and me as well, to an extent. Even after he married and seemed happy, there was always some resentment. But when he noticed his son lacked interest in the things Andrew thought he should pursue, specifically young women, all hell broke loose. He made it crystal clear that it didn't matter what Beckett wanted, that preserving the family power was more important. Decided to line him up for the throne. Got tutors to help increase his magic, his manners, his speech. That poor boy's been through it, all in the name of safeguarding the family's future."

"Beckett can be with who he wants and still be a house ruler. There's no reason that should change."

"Ah, but it will. Andrew's other children are daughters. When they marry and take new names, Beckett will be the only one who can still produce a Chastain heir."

"This entire system is madness," Ros said, half to herself.

"It's a system made to keep power in the same hands, year after year. Still, you defied that system by trying to protect Beckett, and I'm grateful for that."

"Enough that you'll let me go?"

Aggy shook her head fast enough that she didn't even have time to consider it. "I can't do that. Even if I don't take you back to Water house, I can't just let a wanted criminal go free."

"I'm not a criminal, Aggy. I haven't done anything wrong."

"That may be so," Aggy said, "but it's not my place to decide that. I follow the laws of the land—laws your family has helped create—whether or not I agree with them."

Ros knew that was the end of the discussion. Aggy was who she was. No amount of begging or bribery could change a woman like that. As upset as Ros was that they'd been stupid enough to fall in with her, and that she'd trapped them in such an easy fashion, she still respected that the woman had a code that she wouldn't break.

But if she couldn't break Aggy's code, she'd have to figure out how to break Aggy herself.

THE FIELDS HAD TRANSITIONED into bushes and hedges of grand design. Their maker was an artist of the highest order. Periodically Ros would see other things out among the shrubbery, things made of metal and magic-forged. They reminded Ros of the Zoltos and their precise metal magic that allowed them to forge things from the particles of metal in the ground. Despite everything that had transpired, she still had a spot for them in her heart that refused to harden.

While she stared out at the scenery, pretending to be sullen and despondent and, honestly, actually being both of those things, she searched her mind for any bit of training or reading that might get her out of this mess. The only thing she could think of was shadow-walking like Cassian and Brisa, which was far too complicated to even consider trying. Even Cassian's own mother, Ombretta, a powerful Night Elementalist in her own right, couldn't do it. Not only did Ros have zero ideas on how to start such a process, but she also had no idea what would happen if she did it wrong. Still, if it was her only option...

The rumble of hoofbeats caught her ears, distracting her from trying something horribly, terribly foolish. There were four guards on horseback thundering up the road behind them, their armor glinting in the morning sun. Ros saw a flash of green on an armband and the plumed helmet of the lead guard and let out a sigh of relief. They were Earth house guards. Encountering them was still a stroke of bad luck, but at least the riders weren't bandits attacking the wagon. Besides, there was at least a chance they wouldn't recognize this version of her.

"If it weren't for bad luck, I'd have none," Aggy muttered. Her hand crept over and pulled the sleeves of Rosalinde's cloak down to cover the vines holding her in place. "You'll stay quiet if you know what's good for ya."

Ros dipped her head so her hood fell a bit lower as the guards slowed their approach. When she caught sight of the two prisoners the guards held, she knew luck was not on her side. Alaric, bruised but blessedly whole, sat stone-faced atop one of the horses with a small guard at his back.

As much as her heart rose at his presence, it fell as she snuck a glance at Romenia. Ros had never imagined Romenia as a captive instead of the one in charge, but there she was, and the woman was in awful shape. Her nose was broken and blood crusted the side of her face and upper lip, as well as a gash along her temple. Though she was tied up, like Alaric, her sword arm was free from the ropes and cradled in a makeshift sling. There was mud and blood covering so much of her, Ros wasn't sure if she was injured elsewhere, though it was a good sign she was upright and riding the horse.

"You there," the plumed guard said as they came level with Aggy's cart.

Aggy was already slowing before they called her, but now she came to a halt. She didn't bother looking up at the guard, just pursed her lips in evident distaste and asked, "What can I do for ya?"

The guard climbed down from their mount, hand on their sword as they approached the wagon. Ros regarded them from under her hood, trying to look more like a frightened peasant girl than a former queen on the lam. The guard was taller than she was, but not broad. Definitely not the imposing figure that Romenia was when she was in full intimidation mode. She could see brown skin at their neck and on their ungloved hands, but all else was covered. Ros tried to catch a glimpse of the guard's face, but their helmet and her own hood made it an impossibility.

"We're looking for a loose woman," the guard said.

Aggy laughed. "If I had a coin for every time I heard that. Even better, every time I *said* it. Personally, I'd recommend heading down to The Flopping Fish. One of my old haunts, and I hear it's still in good shape, though I haven't been since they changed owners."

"This is no laughing matter," the guard said, though

Ros was nearly certain she heard a smile in their voice. "Have you seen anyone suspicious?"

Aggy lifted her head with measured indignance. "Looking at someone right now."

The guard straightened. "I'm not sure what you mean by that."

"Sure you are," Aggy said. "You guards think you're above the rest of us because the magical nobles have you doing their dirty work, but I bet if you take off that helmet and show your face, I can tell you ten dirty secrets about your grandma and bring you down a peg."

Ros stifled a laugh. She didn't mean to. Aggy's words were just so surprising, and probably accurate, that she couldn't help herself. The strangest part was that Aggy talked about herself as a peasant, but was really working to hide her own nobility, though Ros wasn't sure why.

Laughing was the wrong thing to do. The guard's attention fell on her. "You. Show yourself."

Ros felt Aggy's vines slither away from her, releasing their grip so she could comply with the guard. She reached up and lowered her hood, but kept her eyes downcast from the guard. She'd seen this act plenty of times from the other side of things and it had always bothered her that the magicless felt they had to avert their eyes, but right now she was thankful she could use deference as an excuse not to turn her face to them.

Unfortunately, deference wasn't enough. "Look at me."

Ros drew a steadying breath as she slowly lifted her

head. As soon as her eyes met theirs, the guard said, "It's her."

Ros expected a flurry of movement, weapons drawn, but there was nothing. The guards didn't move, didn't raise their blades, didn't say another word. They just stared at her for a moment while she stared right back.

Finally, Aggy muttered, "Shit or get off the pot."

Her words spurred the guard into action. They drew a dagger from their belt, leaving their sword in its scabbard, and said, "You're coming with us."

Ros didn't argue. She didn't try to run. She knew she could either go with them now or Aggy would turn her in later. Either way, she'd end up in the same place. Summoning as much dignity as she could, Ros climbed down from Aggy's wagon and presented herself to the guard.

The guard tied her hands in front of her, pushed her up onto their horse so her hands were set upon the pommel of the saddle, and guided the horse into a trot. The other guards followed behind as, in the distance, the Earth house walls came into view.

Eleven

T here were more people on the road now. Wagons hauling goods, people pushing carts, carrying bundles, or herding animals. They were coming from the hidden farms Aggy had told her about, Ros assumed, the ones the new fields and flowers had displaced. All were moving in the same direction—the closed gate of Earth house.

"Why is the gate closed?" she asked. She'd never known any house to close their gates in times of peace, and since peace was all Ros had known in her twenty years, the sight of the closed gates sent a nervous trill rushing through her.

She wasn't expecting an answer, so it surprised her when the guard's whisper filled her ear. "Too many mouths and not enough food. They bring in goods to sell, but not crops, which is what we need."

"Can't the Elementalists grow more to feed the people?"

The guard scoffed. "Can they? Yes. Will they? Not when they're ordered to do otherwise."

"That makes little sense."

"Welcome to life outside your castle, princess. Now, keep your head down and your mouth closed. The gate guards aren't as friendly as I am."

The guard raised Rosalinde's hood over her head and when it fell to cover her eyes, she didn't complain. Though she had never been arrested before, and her time on horseback and with guards had always been to gain attention rather than go unnoticed, Ros still recognized that there was something strange about the guard's actions. Bringing in a high priority criminal, as they surely considered her at this point, should give the guards an air of pride. They would be regarded as heroes and probably rewarded. So why were they being so quiet about it? Ros expected them to show their catch to anyone who looked their way, hoping to get a promotion or at least a bit of coin for her capture. Keeping her hidden was suspicious.

As their approach grew even more congested with travelers, one of the other guards riding behind them yelled, "Make way!"

Though she couldn't see the faces of the people they passed because of the hood, she could see their bodies turn to take in the procession and immediately scurry out of the way. Something about these guards in particular seemed to make people nervous. Even Aggy had seemed anxious around them, though she'd done her best to avoid showing it.

A few minutes later, they were sitting in front of the still-closed gates. The guards atop had refused to open for them, or the other citizens gathered outside, citing the need for their commander to give the all clear. Ros noticed a tremble in the man's voice as he had delivered that pronouncement to the guard who sat behind her, but whatever caused it wasn't enough to go against his order to keep the gate locked.

A loud creak scraped through the air around them as the gates opened enough for one rider to come out. The assembly parted with reluctance, and Ros could hear some grumbling about taking a run at the gates when they opened again to let the rider back in. Even with the crowd moving from their path, it took them several minutes to push their way through the packed space. They came directly to Rosalinde's guard. Though she couldn't see either of their faces, Ros could feel the tension between the two guards as soon as the new arrival closed in.

"What the hell are you doing beyond the gate?" the commander asked.

At least, Ros assumed it was the commander. The woman's tone was severe and dripped confidence in a way that few others did. If Ros hadn't known it was a guard speaking, she would've thought her captor was talking to an especially haughty noblewoman.

"Capturing criminals," Rosalinde's guard said, her tone lazy, but just as confident.

"Our orders are to remain inside, gate closed. No exceptions."

"I have different orders."

"No one has *different* orders, because *I* gave the orders."

"My orders came from a higher authority."

The commander sucked in a whistling breath between their teeth. "And whose orders are you following, then? Because I would like a word with them, as you'll find no higher authority in the guard, and I aim to confirm why they're commanding my guards and what fools would dare listen to them."

"You see the plume on my helmet, which means you know who I work for."

"Aye, I see it, but that plume hasn't been given out for some thirty-odd years. Why now, why you, and why wasn't I informed?"

Ros felt the shaky breath inhaled by the guard who held her and was fairly certain she was lying through her teeth. The guard said, "Lady Zolto gave the order on behalf of her brother, the future King of Talabrih, and his betrothed, Queen Elsabet. I am on royal business."

Queen Elsabet, Ros thought, taken aback. She'd known they had named her sister as queen, but the proclamation still seemed shocking when she heard them. Everything was happening so fast and Ros was trapped in the impossibility of fixing things.

There was a brief pause before the commander asked, "Does that mean you have *her*?"

"We are about the Lady's business, Commander Owens. It would serve you well to let us pass."

Ros could hear the challenge in her guard's voice. The commander had surely heard it as well. Though Ros wasn't particularly excited about being taken to *Lady Zolto*, she also wasn't interested in getting stuck between two prideful guards with chips on their shoulders. Neither option was ideal, but maybe there was hope for escape if she got into the city and could distract her guard. Not *much* hope, but more than she had while trapped between these two women weighing each other's worth.

After too long a moment, the commander relented. She called to the guards on top of the wall, saying, "Let them through."

They forced their way through the crowd still trying to gain entrance to the city. Though the people on both sides begged and pleaded with the guards to let them in, the women moved toward the gates as if they couldn't hear them. And maybe they couldn't. Saul had been concerned about the invisibility of the magicless in the kingdom, and though she was loath to admit anything he said had merit, Ros was witnessing their neglect with her own eyes.

They entered Earth house's gates and continued down the main street. It was a wide lane lined with blossoming fruit trees and decorative vases full of ever-blooming spelled flowers. The colors were magnificent; the streets practically glowed with every shade conceivable, and some she'd never dared to imagine.

The street was perfumed with memories. Living with one of the greatest Earth house mages in living history, their home had always been full of young Botanicals looking for guidance. The queen had always taken the most promising under her wing, nurturing and guiding them to become more than they ever could've on their own. The scents that poured through the castle had been as varied and lovely as the mages who produced them. Now, those same aromas paraded through nose, reminding Ros of all the good her mother had done through the years.

As they passed under the branch of a peach tree, Ros caught a whiff of sweetness rolling past. It smelled fruity and floral. Familiar.

She swallowed. It wasn't a peach tree she had smelled; it was peonies. Not just peonies, but the specific variation she had grown accustomed to over the years, the one that underlined every lesson the queen had given to promising Botanical mages. Ros could pluck that scent from her memories at will.

She knew with sudden certainty that the guards weren't taking her to the Zoltos; no, they were taking her to see her mother.

THE GUARDS TURNED off the main street and wound their way through the city on a serpentine path. Though Ros had been to Earth house before, she'd never left the main road. It smelled different here. Less sweet, more sweat. A whiff of livestock hit her as they turned another corner, and a low braying filled her ears. She heard voices in the street ahead, followed by a rush of words, then the closing of doors. Though she couldn't be sure what was happening with the hood still over her head, she thought the approach of her guards had sent people off the street and out of their path.

Who were these guards?

The turns they'd taken had left her thoroughly lost. Ros knew that even if she tried to form an escape plan now, she wouldn't get far. Her nose might lead her back to the main road, but then what? Her friends would still be trapped, and the only place she could run would be the Lady Ruler's house. That wasn't an option.

After about ten minutes of walking through unfamiliar territory, the guards stopped and climbed from their horses. The plumed guard grabbed Rosalinde's restraints and pulled her down from the mount. She secured the beast to a post, then dragged Ros through even more alleys and side streets, stopping every few feet to check for people milling about or to make sure the area was clear. It again struck Rosalinde as odd that the people who had outmaneuvered the highest commander in the Earth house guard were sneaking them through the town instead of parading them in front of Lady Valeria.

After another fifteen minutes of sneaking around, they finally reached their destination. The guards shoved Ros and her companions into a dim room with windows so dingy it looked like the sun had set, despite it being midday. The guard who hadn't had a passenger on their horse made their way around to each of the prisoners, cutting their bonds. As soon as Alaric was free, he ran to her.

Ros threw her arms around his neck and he picked her up, whispering her name against her chopped hair. When he sat Ros on her feet, she pulled back to look at his banged up, smiling, handsome face. She returned his smile, unable to help herself.

A dozen things flew through her head, but before she could say any of them, Alaric leaned forward and pressed his lips to hers. It wasn't the dangerous kisses she'd had with them while they were sneaking around, or the eager ones while he tried to get under her skirts. It wasn't even like the last one they'd shared when she'd been able to feel his love pouring through his kiss. No, this kiss said he was happy she was okay, that he had felt lost without her, that he'd been terrified of what Aggy might have done, and, maybe, that he didn't want to be away from her again.

Ros recognized all those things in the mere seconds it took for her to pull away. Though she did pull away, there was a part of her that had reciprocated those same feelings to Alaric through that kiss. She'd been afraid of what could've happened to him and delighted to know he was okay, even if he was just as trapped as she was.

She heard one guard clear their throat, and she spun toward them. All four stood just a few feet away, stock-still, staring at Ros and Alaric. Her fists balled at her side before she realized what she was doing. It was bad enough that she had to sort out feelings for Alaric on top of everything that was already happening, but to do it in front of these people was too much.

"Enjoying the show?" she asked.

"I've seen better," one of them said. "I've probably been more entertaining with it myself, honestly. But work with what you've got."

Ros was readying to tear into them when they took off their helmet. It was Florian.

Her jaw nearly dropped to the floor. Ros closed the gap between them and threw herself against her friend. Never in her life had she been so happy to see one of the arrogant house ruler's heirs.

"You're not going to kiss me now, are you? We've already been through that, and I'd rather not repeat it. No offense."

Ros swatted his shoulder, ignoring the heat that crept into her cheeks at the mention of her brief kiss with Florian. It had meant nothing to either of them, and she certainly had no intention of ever doing it again, but that didn't make the memory any less steamy. Florian was a lot of things, and not all of them pleasant, but she could say with assurance that he was a fantastic kisser.

She pushed aside the thought, and Florian slipped past her to go to Romenia's side. Ros watched as he cradled the brutish woman's face with an unabashed tenderness. He muttered under his breath as he wiped at the caked on blood and dirt. Romenia stared up at him through swollen, bloodshot eyes, but even with the damage marring her face, Ros could see that there was a gentleness in her expression as she saw Florian's concern for her.

Ros turned from the sight, feeling almost as if she were intruding on a significant moment between them that neither had seen coming. She turned to the other guards. She expected Beckett to remove his helmet next, and thank the elements she had no memory of a kiss to fight where he was concerned. It wasn't Beckett, though; instead, it was Brisa. Ros gave her a nod and said, "Glad you made it."

"Me too," she said. "Though you are looking a little worse for wear."

Ros forced a smile as she ran her hands over what was left of her hair. "It's been an interesting two days."

When the guard who'd been holding her removed the plumed helmet, Rosalinde's mouth went dry. She stared at the woman, her former friend, unsure what to say or think or feel. Larkin had betrayed her, had sentenced her to a life with a man she didn't love, all as a play for power within the kingdom. Despite her cryptic assurances that she was trying to do what was best for the kingdom, Ros had seen the way Larkin acted when she thought she could get away with it, and she hadn't liked it one bit. It didn't matter what Larkin said at this point, or even that she'd had a hand in rescuing Ros—the woman could not be trusted.

It only took a second for Ros to settle on this conclusion and turn away from Larkin. Her eyes fell to the last guard as they took off their helmet.

With a jolt of surprise, Rosalinde's gaze met the dark stare of Cassian Scalise.

Twelve

Cassian stared at her, his face a tight mask that revealed no emotion. The last time she'd seen him, Ros had told an assembled crowd she was choosing Lyzandor Zolto as her betrothed instead of him. Now, he had just witnessed her kissing her ex-lover. Not that she'd had a choice. Alaric had done that all on his own. But Ros hadn't exactly protested.

All that really mattered was how Cassian saw it. When she'd first met him, she'd been amazed at how he allowed his emotions to show freely on his face, how he somehow gained confidence from letting others know exactly what he was thinking. Ros had grown accustomed to secret motives and hidden agendas with the nobles, and even her own family, so Cassian's openness was refreshing, albeit surprising. Now, though, with the blank expression he wore, Ros wasn't sure what he thought.

"Cassian," she breathed, explanations flitting through her mind. "Let me explain—"

He held up a hand. "There's no time to do whatever it is you think you need to do."

"But I—"

"Stop," he said. "You don't owe me anything."

Despite his words, Cassian's eyes trailed over her face as if he was searching for answers. Her face, then, was *not* as emotionless as his. She tried to speak to him through her eyes, the set of her jaw, the tremble in her lips. Cassian read her like a book, but his grim expression did not falter.

"Please, just give me a few minutes and I can explain everything."

"What do you need to explain to this guy, anyway?" Alaric asked, sidling up next to her and putting his arm around Rosalinde's waist.

Ros pulled away from him instantly, but not before Cassian's face briefly twisted into a scowl, then righted itself again. She turned to Alaric, who wore his hurt like a mantle. Gods, she didn't want to cause either of them pain!

Ros sighed. "If we can just take a breath…"

"I don't understand," Alaric said, brows knitted together. "Your sister said you were *forced* to choose a husband. That you'd done what was necessary. So what does this guy have to do with any of that?"

"Because she was going to choose the Night mage if it hadn't been for me," Larkin said.

They all turned their eyes on her. Even Ros, who knew the role Larkin had played, was surprised at her declaration. The words seemed to lift a weight from Rosalinde's shoulders, as if revealing that truth had set her free.

"What?" Alaric said, eyes wide. "I thought you chose Zolto because you *had* to, and he was a safe choice since you've known him forever. I didn't know you *wanted* to choose someone, especially not someone you just met. We've been together for two years—" Ros tried to interrupt, but he held up a hand and continued. "I know, those two years were secret. They weren't everything they could've been, but you can't lie and tell me you felt nothing for me. I *know* better. Maybe you didn't love me, but it wasn't as meaningless to you as you want me to believe."

Ros swallowed. "No, it wasn't meaningless."

"Then how could you balk at the idea of being with me, someone you know and care for, someone who would hang the moon for you, but you're willing to throw your heart at someone you just met? You wanted to choose some stranger?"

Cassian's words were clipped out through his clenched jaw. "She didn't want to choose me. If she had, she would have. This woman doesn't love me, if that's what you're worried about. If she did, she would have trusted that whatever mess was going on, I would help her get through it."

Alaric's hurt expression hardened as he turned to face

Cassian. "Will you? Is that something you can magically do after knowing her for a few weeks? You've somehow been able to deduce all her hopes and dreams and needs? That's some trick, mage."

"Don't hurl words at me just because you're angry. I am not the one who hurt you. I was just a distraction for your beloved while she tried to figure out what to do when her charmed life fell to pieces."

"That's not what you were to me," Ros said.

"Then what was I?" Cassian asked. Though his face was emotionless and his tone dripped venom, she could hear the hurt underneath, and the desperation to know if he really meant something to her.

"You weren't anything," Alaric said, "except a waste of her time, a foolish mistake, a placeholder. I'm the one she's been sneaking secret moments and sharing her hopes with. I'm the one who will take care of her when she needs it, no matter what. You're just a pretty boy who charmed his way under her skirts before the others could."

"Whoa now," Florian said, rejoining them after checking on Romenia. He stepped between Alaric and Cassian. "Everyone needs to calm down."

Alaric's face burned with anger as he turned on Florian. "What's it to you, anyway? Trying to make us look bad and turn yourself into a viable option for her? You've already admitted to kissing her."

Florian's brows shot up. "I'm just trying to keep the peace, friend."

"You are no friend of mine. And you," he said, pointing at Ros, "I can't believe how easily you'd fall into bed with some random man just because he's on daddy's approved list. I love you, and I have for a long time, but this..." he trailed off, waving a hand at Cassian and Florian.

"Your tone doesn't illustrate the love you speak of," Florian said. "Just because you've been involved for a while doesn't mean she owes you anything."

"Stay out of this," Alaric and Cassian both said. The two men looked at each other then, as if they were each appalled at agreeing with something the other said.

"Fascinating as this is," Brisa cut in with a tone that did not sound fascinated at all, "we've got a lot more to worry about right now than who our buxom heroine wants to bone."

Ros ignored her, saying, "It's not like that. None of what you think—"

"It doesn't matter," Cassian interrupted. "Brisa is right. We have a lot to do and squabbling will get us nowhere."

Ros grit her teeth to keep from saying what she wanted to. *Squabbling? That's what he thinks this is?*

She'd spent the last few weeks trying to keep herself busy so she wouldn't think about him constantly. Ros had imagined the conversation over and over, trying to guess which way it would go. Most of the time it ended up with her in Cassian's arms, sometimes it ended with him unable to forgive her when she was in an especially sour mood, but never did it end with him ignoring the actual facts of what had happened between them and saying it was nothing more than *squabbling*. At least Alaric had the decency to be honest about their history, even if it was a past that was muddled and confusing.

"Fine," she said.

Cassian winced. Ros wasn't sure if it was her tone, or if he had expected something else from her. Maybe he wanted something else, maybe he wanted the explanation that he'd refused, or for her to beg for his forgiveness, but she couldn't read his mind. If she could, she still wasn't sure she'd be able to satisfy him. And Brisa wasn't wrong; time was running out.

"Great, so let's figure out what we're going to do next," Brisa said. "We'll need a plan when the rest of the Rising Tide arrives."

"The rest of them?" Ros asked.

Brisa looked at her like she'd sprouted a second head. "Do you expect a revolution with just the seven of us?"

"I don't know what to expect, since no one ever wants to tell me what's going on," Ros said.

"Maybe there's a reason for that," Brisa smirked.

"You're out of line," Cassian growled.

Brisa's smirk faded instantly, and she muttered, "Apologies."

Ros noticed the way Brisa fell in line with Cassian without question. She wasn't sure why someone from the Delos Santos line would obey the words of a Night mage without even the slightest hesitation, even if he was from the ruling house family. If the rest of the kingdom knew she even existed, she would be elevated to royalty, if she wanted to be or not. There had to be something more to their relationship.

Maybe Brisa was in love with him. That would explain her dislike of Ros and her deference to Cassian.

Before she could dwell on it further, Florian piped in, "The basics, then?"

After the anger and hostility of the last few minutes, Ros was so grateful for his upbeat tone that she nearly laughed out loud. She remembered the exact moment in the woods with Florian when she realized that she not only liked him, but that she could be friends with him. Now, she was beginning to cherish that blooming friendship more and more. There were still hurdles for them to overcome, but she felt they were on the right track.

With a nod from Ros, Florian said, "Your sister is the Queen of Talabrih, but after the meeting with the house rulers and the mess that turned into, you already knew it was going that way. Now it's official, and she's betrothed to Lyzandor Zolto to hold up your end of the marriage agreement."

"Zandor does not know what's going on behind the scenes," Larkin cut in.

"Unlikely," Brisa said with a roll of her eyes.

"I'm serious. I've kept him out of it so he wouldn't be tied to this... this... treason," she spat.

Cassian said, "It seems highly improbable that he could stay out of it, considering all that's happened.

However, Zandor seems like a decent fellow, even if we have had our own previous disagreements."

Florian pursed his lips. "Dubious, at best. But how about we meet in the middle and say he has little knowledge and less input?"

Larkin nodded. "He's suspicious of what's happening, but uninvolved."

Florian turned back to Ros. "Your mother is trying to use Elsabet as a puppet to control the throne from behind the scenes."

"No surprise there," Ros said.

"And no surprise that it isn't working. Elsabet is far too strong-willed for that, even if she is playing to your mother's desires," Larkin said, a fondness for Elsa clear in her voice.

Florian said, "Well, here's a doozy for you: the Queen Mother is also engaged."

"What?" Ros spat. "My father has been missing for a few weeks and she's marrying that Earth house lover of hers?"

Florian swallowed. "Not someone from Earth house, actually." In a whisper, he added, "I'll need you to dish on the Earth house lover when it's a more appropriate time."

"Well then, who the hell is she marrying?"

Cassian's dark eyes turned darker still as he said, "My brother."

IT TOOK Ros several minutes to compose herself after treating the group to a vast array of expletives, both common and extraordinarily complicated. When she calmed down, she turned her gaze to Larkin. The darkness she had seen in the other girl's eyes in the courtyard was gone. Ros assumed that was thanks to Cassian, but something about the situation made her hesitant to ask in front of the others. She could wait until she had a moment alone with him so as not to add even more for her friends to worry about on top of everything else. Besides, asking in front of the group would reveal one of Cassian's secrets; though some had seen him helping the medic full of darkness, Ros wasn't sure who was privy to how much information, and she didn't want to give him away if he wasn't ready to.

Instead, she asked her former friend, "What does this have to do with your plan?"

Larkin looked taken aback. "*My* plan?"

"To take the throne."

"I don't have a plan to take the throne."

"Okay, then the plan of whoever you're working for."

Larkin put her hands on her hips in a way that told Rosalinde she had almost reached her nonsense limit. Ros had seen that expression dozens of times through the years, but never directed at her.

"My presence here should indicate where my allegiance is."

"I don't know why you're here," Ros said. "You were my best friend until you blackmailed me into choosing your brother as my betrothed. Or I thought you were, at least. I guess I don't really know who you are or what to think about the things you've done."

Larkin's eyes grew wide. "Are you serious right now? That's really what you've been thinking these last few weeks?"

"What was I supposed to think?"

"You were supposed to trust me. Like I would've trusted you. Like I have been trusting you my entire life."

"You haven't *known* me your entire life," Ros said, rolling her eyes.

"We may not have been friends the whole time, but you can bet I knew who the future queen of Talabrih was from the moment I was able to understand such things. As your subject, I believed you could do anything. As your friend, I knew you'd do it with kindness. I've been trusting you to make this kingdom better for as long as I knew it was possible. Don't tell me my faith was misplaced."

She didn't know what, if anything, any of Larkin's professions meant. It didn't change the note she found in her room in Larkin's handwriting, telling her to choose Earth house to keep her father alive. It didn't change the way the Zoltos had paraded around the castle as if they were untouchable, doing anything they pleased.

No matter how flowery or inspirational Larkin got with her words, Ros had seen the darkness inside her when she'd tried to send Beckett home. She might fool the others, but Ros wasn't buying her innocent act.

Ros held up her hand where her father's drop of blood still formed an arrow on her skin. "If you're really on my side, why are you still keeping my father prisoner?"

"I'm not keeping him prisoner, I'm keeping him safe. As soon as I found out he was missing, I sent our best scouts looking for him. They found him wandering through the woods as if under a spell. So, they brought him back to Earth house for his own protection. The Lady Ruler has him in a guest room under guard because they haven't been able to break the spell. I didn't get a chance to tell you all this because you were out with the Elementalists when we found him, and I wasn't sure which of them I could trust. For all I knew," she said, casting a suspicious glance at Cassian, "one of them was responsible."

By the glare Cassian returned, it seemed as if neither of them trusted the other. It irked Ros to see the distrust from Larkin's side, considering Cassian wasn't the one who seemed to be conniving to get his brother on the throne. Though he was mysterious and maybe a bit brooding, it was Larkin's actions that were condemning, not his.

Ros said, "And what about after? You didn't bother saying anything about my father, instead letting me accept the throne while forcing me to choose your brother. If you'd really been trying to help, there was plenty of time to talk when I got back."

"Was there? You were always surrounded by guards. I sent you half a dozen letters with a different servant each time and they were all returned unopened. I didn't know what had turned you against me or why you'd refuse my letters. All I knew was that there was something going on that was beyond my comprehension, and I had to do what little I could for you, your father, and the kingdom."

Ros remembered her sister saying much of the same regarding the letters. Someone, or many someones, had kept her from receiving those messages. She wondered who had received them instead and what information they had gleaned from them, but she didn't have time to dwell on that now. "Fine. If that's the truth, take me to him."

Brisa sighed, cutting through the back and forth between the two former friends. "You two are taking forever. Just kiss and make up already. Do you not understand what I mean when I say we don't have time for this? Because what I mean is *we don't have time for this*."

"What is so urgent that we can't work this out?" Ros asked.

As if in answer, the door behind them crashed open and Water house guards poured through the opening. There were enough of them to encircle the motley band of rebels in a ring three soldiers deep. The guards pointed spears and swords at Rosalinde's group, and though they could overpower some guards with their elemental magic, they certainly didn't have the numbers to fight the two dozen mages who filed in after them.

"Seems a little heavy-handed, don't you think?" Florian asked, raising his hands in surrender.

"Perhaps, but you've already slipped through our fingers once before."

The voice was cold, distant. It wasn't like the one who had read Ros bedtime stories or sang her sweet songs when she was a child. But as she stepped into the dim room and a mote of sunlight shone through the dirty windows as if to give her a spotlight, there was no doubt that the beautiful Earth house mage standing there was Rosalinde's mother.

Thirteen

Ros stared at the Queen Mother. Her emotions were running rampant through her body and she knew without a shadow of a doubt that her face couldn't hide the things she felt, especially the betrayal that seemed to win every battle as the other emotions vied for attention. Heat flared through her as she thought of all the things that had happened over the last few weeks, and suddenly the betrayal by those she held dearest turned to a white-hot rage.

"We need to talk," Sariyah said, lips pursed.

There was no hint of her feelings, no sign of guilt, or anger, or even delight at catching her prey. Ros marveled at the way she stood there with her face as smooth as a statue. Through the years, Ros had always wanted to be like her mother in that regard, but looking at her now, she was thankful that she ended up more like her father.

Screwing up her courage while trying to pretend that

her mother's presence wasn't a thorn in her side, Ros said, "I don't think that's necessary."

A tiny crease formed at the inside of Sariyah's right eyebrow, the only indication she wasn't made of stone. "Are you under the delusion that you have a choice in the matter? I can rid you of that misconception right now, if you'd like."

With a slight nod of her head, the innermost guards tightened their circle around Rosalinde's group. One of them stepped out of line and moved toward Larkin, but Sariyah said, "Not her. She's one of mine."

Rosalinde's eyes cut daggers at Larkin, who looked completely shocked at the Queen Mother's words. It didn't matter what Larkin tried to say at this point. Ros wouldn't be fooled by her again, especially now that her mother had just admitted to pulling Larkin's strings. It explained how Sariyah had found them so easily, and why Larkin had postponed their departure with her escalating falsehoods.

Well, she could lie as much as she wanted, but she would not get back in Rosalinde's good graces. The chasm between them was too deep, the foundation of their friendship completely demolished.

The guard lunged toward Florian instead, kicking the Fire mage's legs out from under him. Florian hit the ground and tried to rise, but another guard stepped forward and held his sword tip at Florian's throat.

Florian tilted his neck to give them a better angle. His lips curled back in a magnificent snarl. "Do it then."

"Don't tempt me, lordling," the guard growled.

Florian's eyes moved from the guard to the Queen Mother. "Another will rise in my place. And another. And a third. We will not rest until the true queen is restored."

Ros couldn't stop her eyes from going to Brisa for the briefest second, but they slid back to her mother as the tip of the sword against Florian's neck drew blood. "Stop this. Now."

Sariyah held up a hand, and the guards stepped back. "I think she gets the point."

"Why are you doing this?" Ros asked. "This isn't who you are."

"Are you certain, dove? It isn't as if we were ever close."

The words stung Ros, sending tears unbidden to the corners of her eyes. "What could I have done to change that? I was a child, and you were my whole world, but I always knew I wasn't enough for you. Why?"

Sariyah ignored her questions and turned her back to Ros. As the Queen Mother stepped outside, two guards flanked by four Elementalists grabbed Rosalinde's arms and pulled her out of the building behind Sariyah.

They followed the queen into a waiting litter, where they hoisted Ros through the curtains and onto the bed inside. Her mother was already reclined on a pile of pillows, plucking a date from a tray. As the litter started moving, Sariyah said, "Are you hungry, darling? You must be famished after all that foolishness running through the woods. For all the good it did you. You're back in my clutches yet again."

Ros scowled at her. "I'm fine. Not that you actually care."

"Don't pout. You'll age your face prematurely. You know that."

Ros furrowed her brows. This woman sounded nothing like the one she'd known her whole life. It was true that Ros had always been closer to her father, while Elsabet had been their mother's shadow, but Sariyah had never been so blatantly cold to her before. "What do you want from me? And don't pretend you're here for my wellbeing."

"You've got the wrong impression of things, my sweet, and I'm here to set it right. You ran from the castle as if you're a common criminal, when that couldn't be further from the truth."

"I don't believe you," Ros said.

"It doesn't really matter what you believe," Sariyah said. "The truth is all that matters. Do you know what the truth of this whole debacle is?"

"No," Ros breathed, surprising herself when she realized she truly didn't understand how things had devolved to this.

Sariyah smiled, but Ros saw it for what it was: an animal baring its teeth. Sariyah was a viper poised to strike.

And strike she did.

So fast that Ros didn't even see her move, Sariyah's

fingers sent thorny vines slithering over Rosalinde's skin. They bit into her flesh, pinpricks of pain that grew numb almost instantly. The numbness spread through Rosalinde's body until she couldn't move any part of her except her eyes.

Ros tried to reach for her magic, but she couldn't find it within her. It was as if the thorns had numbed the magic inside her, too.

"The truth is whatever I say it is," Sariyah said, her eyes as black as midnight. "So if I say my daughter was corrupted by an evil Elementalist hellbent on having the kingdom as his own, then that's the truth. If my poor daughter couldn't be saved no matter how hard I fought for her very soul and, in a fit of rage, she attacked me and I had to use my magic against her or be killed... Well then, the whole of Talabrih will mourn with me. So, right now I say we go find a nice, quiet place where no one will hear your screams, and we'll figure out the truth together. Today, my daughter, is your day to die."

ROS LAID on the floor of the litter in silence, unable to stir in the slightest, watching her mother eat from a tray of dates, berries, and cheeses. She watched Sariyah pick up a handful of blueberries and toss them into her mouth indelicately.

Though Ros had suspected that her mother was under the influence of the darkness, this was the moment she knew it was much, much more. The others had said Sariyah was engaged to a man full of darkness; they didn't realize she was *becoming* the darkness.

"You don't like blueberries," Ros mumbled. Her lips and tongue were frozen along with the rest of her, but her words were clear enough to be understood.

Her mother—or rather, the *thing* wearing her mother's body—looked at the remaining blueberries on the plate. "Thank you. I'll need to remember that for the future. Shame, really. They're quite good."

"How long?" Ros asked, barely able to get the words out.

"There are so many things you could mean by that. How long have I been playing this part? How long have I been planning to murder you? How long will your friends survive inside that burning building?"

As if in response to her words, a bell chimed in the distance and Ros could hear the shouts behind them as people ran to put out the flames. Ros wanted to reach across the litter and grab her mother, the darkness, by the throat. But what had she expected? That her friends would be safe once she left with her mother? That was foolishness. But then, Ros was a fool. No one was safe if they were on her side.

At least if the darkness killed her, she couldn't get anyone else hurt. Not that it was a consolation, when several people she cared about were dying right now, and all she could do was lie on the floor and try not to choke on her own tongue.

They traveled in silence for a while, the tinkling bells fading as they moved farther away until Ros could no longer hear the tolling melody marking her friends' deaths. Ros was unable to find words for the pain she was feeling at the loss of her companions. Most of them were powerful mages, so there was a tiny sliver of herself that wanted to hang onto the hope that they'd made it out, but hope had done little for her lately. As much as she wanted them to live, there was still the knowledge that she wouldn't see them again, not if her mother had her way. The darkness seemed content in the silence, having their fill of blueberries, staining her mother's lips deep purple.

When they stopped moving, Ros expected the dark queen to get out of the litter. Or maybe they would have one of their guards retrieve Ros from inside. Instead, they just sat there, curtains closed to a world on fire.

After several minutes, the dark queen asked, "What would you do if I let you go?" Without waiting for an attempt at an answer, they continued, "Probably more of the same. You seemed determined to undermine my plans at every turn. It pains me to say that, you know, because you seem to just stumble into these situations with no forethought. I'm not sure if you've just been falling into lucky breaks or if you actually have some wits about you. Personally, I think it's the former, but either way, you've thwarted me too many times to keep taking chances. I have been actively planning this takeover for years, and you will not keep me from it."

Ros had no idea why the dark queen was confiding all this to her. Perhaps because they knew she'd be dead in a few minutes. Or maybe they were lonely at the top, unable to share their endeavors with anyone, because so few knew what they really were. Whatever the reason, she wanted to keep them talking. It might only prolong her life for a little while longer, but there was at least a chance that her paralysis would wear off and she'd be able to make some sort of escape.

"Maybe you're not good at planning," Ros mumbled.

The dark queen leveled a stare at her that would've set Ros trembling if her body had been under her control. "Do you think this is easy? Taking over a corrupt monarchy doesn't come with a guidebook. At every turn, I'm faced with a slew of fools and sycophants with no real ambition or drive. These people only want power for bragging rights. They don't understand there is so much more."

"You'll teach them?"

The darkness waved a perfectly manicured hand. "Waste of time. I have better things to do once I get my plan back on track. After you impeded my first initiative, I started making things up as I went. Hence, taking your mother's body. I *really* did not want to jump in here. She makes *me* seem warm and cuddly, and I tried to murder my whole family."

"She's a good person," Ros replied, though she was saying it more for herself than the dark queen. Ros wanted to believe that her mother had loved her in her own way, even if she hadn't always been the mother Ros needed.

"Good. Bad. It's relative. You want to believe she's good because that means there's a chance to redeem her and your silly little brain still thinks you're getting out of this alive. Two things you should know with regard to that: first, I dosed you with a poison that has a long incubation, so there's no chance it will wear off anytime soon; second, after living in your mother for the last few weeks, I can assure you that she is not a good person. Might as well wipe that hope from your mind right now. There's nothing left to redeem."

Ros let the words tumble around in her mind for a moment. There was a chance the dark queen was telling the truth; however, there was also a chance they were lying, as Gaius had been when he said he was the sole survivor of Night house. She had witnessed the darkness telling lies and truths, but still couldn't determine which they were doing right now.

The dark queen suddenly grabbed the curtain and rubbed it against her lips, leaving the blueberry stain on the fabric. She yelled, "Kalin."

A guard appeared almost instantly. "Yes, Your Highness?"

"Take this traitor into the woods and execute her."

There was a slight hesitation in the guard's response. Perhaps he was surprised that the Queen Mother had just ordered her own daughter murdered, or that there was to be an execution without a trial in front of the house council. Whatever the reason he paused, it passed.

Kalin reached for Rosalinde's arms to lift her up, but the dark queen said, "No, silly. Make it hurt."

The guard swallowed, but there was no hesitation this time as he took hold of Rosalinde's newly shortened hair and pulled her from the litter. Ros could feel the pressure on the top of her head, but for one brief moment she was grateful her mother's poison was still working to numb her mistreated scalp.

The guard threw her on the ground. When she didn't move, he tried to stand her up, not seeming to realize she had no control over her body. She crashed into the dirt. Ros heard some of the other guards snickering and she wasn't sure if it was the sorry state of her body or the struggle the guard was having hauling her back up. Either way, no one moved to help them.

She thought he might pick her up and throw her over his shoulder, but no. He was under direct orders to cause her pain. The dark queen must get some sick pleasure from forcing others to do her perverse will, or she was enjoying seeing the turmoil in him at the task he was assigned, for there was no other reason she would demand he treat Ros this way when she couldn't feel the pain he inflicted.

Whether Kalin realized she couldn't feel the pain or not, Ros wasn't sure. After a moment of uncertainty, Kalin opted to leave Ros on the ground and pull her by the ankles. She stared at the sky as he dragged her over rocks and roots. It was bright blue now, the overcast morning giving way to a cheerfully bright afternoon.

Ros felt there was something odd about being dragged to her death on a perfect day. Didn't the world understand that she was about to die? Didn't it care? Instead of a soft breeze, warm sunlight, and a clear sky, there should be whipping winds, dark clouds, and fat drops of rain that chilled to the bone.

The first droplet hit her cheek as soon as the thought entered her mind. It drifted up toward her temple as Kalin dragged her, creating a rivulet as cold as a snowflake. Or at least she *thought* it was cold. Maybe that was just in her head. The first drop could have been mistaken for a tear streaking her face, if not for those that followed. They pelted down from an empty sky, rattling out a tune against Kalin's armor.

He was muttering something, but Ros couldn't hear what. The deep bass of his voice was a rumble of harmony in the song the rain created. A few minutes later, he dragged her under the shelter of a group of trees. They were woven together at the top, too precise to be natural, but beautiful all the same. Kalin dropped her feet to the ground and stood over her, his shoulder-length blond hair curling at the ends and dripping wet.

"Are you doing that?" he asked. Then, in a mumble to himself, he added, "She shouldn't be able to do anything but breathe in this state. What a mess."

Ros didn't answer. She could have probably groaned out some nonsense between numb lips, but there wasn't a point to it. This man had dragged her out here to kill her. She didn't have the energy or the ability to satisfy his desire for conversation in her last moments. The one consolation she had was that he seemed a good sort, despite the task assigned to him, and the worst he would do was murder her.

He pulled a dagger from his belt. Ros found a strange satisfaction that her body couldn't show fear at the end of her days. Though it was through none of her own doing, she still found comfort in it, making her less afraid than she otherwise would have been.

Kalin sighed and dropped the blade into the dirt beside her before plopping on the ground by her head. "I hope they get here soon. I don't want to leave you alone while you're like this, but if I'm gone too long, your mother will get suspicious."

Ros stared up at the man. Though her face didn't register her confusion, her mind did. She was waiting for death from a man who would not deliver it. But why? Who was he waiting for?

The rain pouring down outside their tree covering slowed, then stopped. Kalin smiled and said, "So it *was* you doing that. Very handy trick if you're trying to annoy someone."

He picked at a blade of grass between his knees and said, "You're probably wondering what's going on, and I bet if you could ask, you would."

"Why?"

"Why?" he repeated, brows furrowed. "Why what?"

"Wait."

Kalin's face broadened in a smile again, all teeth. "Why wait? Well, I don't really have much choice. I mean, I guess I could cover you up with some branches and hope you stay undiscovered. Or discovered, depending on who comes by. This whole undercover business is confusing. Anyway, let's just say my employer would be upset with me if I let you die."

"Who?" Ros croaked.

"The Queen of Talabrih, of course," he said with a conspiratorial wink. "I work for your sister."

Fourteen

~~~

Ros seemed to be thanking the elements for her sister more and more as of late, and growing further indebted to her with each passing day. Now she could add her sister's network of spies and employees to her list of things to be grateful for, even if Kalin seemed more brawn than brain. Though Ros had never considered the need for such things, she was relieved that her little sister had been thinking ahead when she hired Kalin, and whoever else might work for her. A well-placed guard certainly came in handy in a pinch.

"Ah, there they are," Kalin said, rising to his feet.

Ros heard footsteps approaching, but she couldn't turn to see who it was. A second later, two heads leaned over in unison and she felt her heart jolt against her ribs as Beckett and Teague came into view.

"I have to get back," Kalin said. "Do you have the blood?"

Beckett said, "Right here. I'll help you with it."

They stepped away for a moment, and when they returned, Kalin's hands were slick with red. "It was nice meeting you," he said as he dragged the red down the front of his legs. "I hope I'll have a chance to serve you again under better circumstances."

He gave her one last bright smile and vanished from her view.

"I can't believe that guy was your first," Beckett muttered.

"Everyone has one," Teague said. He picked up Rosalinde's arm and inspected the marks where the thorns had bitten into her skin.

Beckett huffed. "Right, but does he have to go around being so cheerful and good looking?"

Ros wanted to laugh. After everything that had happened today, Beckett's casual remark about Teague's sex life felt like a soothing balm for her chapped soul. She glanced at Teague from the corner of her eyes and saw that he was doing a poor job of suppressing a smile while he checked on Rosalinde's condition.

"You think he's handsome, then?"

"Obviously," Beckett said. Then, thinking better of it, he added, "I mean, if you like chiseled perfection or whatever."

"And you do?"

"I'm not the one whose conquests are under review—"

"Yet," Teague cut in.

Beckett's face was unreadable from Rosalinde's current position on the ground, but the silence seemed to say he wasn't fond of that idea.

"We can all agree that he's attractive. He scored you, didn't he? I bet he can't walk ten paces without finding a man who would—"

"I can hear you," Ros muttered.

Both men's eyes snapped to hers. A stunned second later, Beckett said, "Forgive us, My Queen. We didn't realize you were conscious."

Without waiting for a response, and without even the slightest sign of embarrassment regarding their conversation, Teague's medical curiosity kicked in. "Can you tell us what happened to you?"

She was trying to force out the words when the sudden slap of feet against the ground caught her ears. Ros croaked out words at them, tried to tell them to run. These men were not fighters, and she didn't want someone else to die on her behalf. Whether or not they heard her, she couldn't say, but they didn't move. They stayed at her side, Beckett with hands raised in defense and Teague putting himself between her and whatever approached.

Ros saw the moment their tension faded. Beckett's arms fell back to his side and Teague, one of the most serious mages Ros had ever met, smiled. A few seconds later, a filthy, soot-streaked face peered down at her and she thought her heart would explode from the sheer beauty of it.

She wanted to say his name, wanted to scream and cry and laugh because he was alive. Alive!

Cassian, Cassian, Cassian.

"She's completely immobilized," Teague replied to Cassian's unasked question. "We were just trying to work out what happened when we heard you approaching."

Cassian shook his head. "We need to go, now. I don't know the details, but I saw a squad of guards on their way here. They're the reason I found you as quickly as I did."

"We can take her back to the barn," Beckett said.

"No time," Cassian replied. He kneeled and picked Ros up from the ground, tossing her over his shoulder. "Hold on to me."

Ros wanted to make a snarky comment about not being able to hold on to anything, but Beckett and Teague grabbed hold of him and Ros realized his words had been for them. A second later, they were walking through the brightly colored world between shadows. Ros closed her eyes for a second, imagining she could dance in the pink and purple fields of this place, dreaming of being able to move at all.

Time felt thick here, as if it was full of impossibilities, and as if it moved slower than in reality. She knew they were only there for seconds, but it seemed like so much longer as she stared at the strange, alien landscape in wonder. It differed from the times she'd shadow-walked with him before somehow—no less beautiful, but Ros felt a quiet sadness about this in-between place that she hadn't noticed before.

When the color faded, they were in an empty charred clearing in the middle of the woods. As Cassian turned to make sure they were alone, Ros recognized where they'd landed. They were standing in the Night Cradle.

Cassian laid her back on the ground, and a sudden rush of nausea washed through her. The air filling her lungs grew hard to breathe. Beckett and Teague came to her side, neither of them seeming to notice the heaviness clinging to the surrounding air.

"You have the Night in you," Cassian said, his voice sounding like a faraway dream. "Let it help you."

Ros remembered the way Gaius had guided her when she'd been here before. She let herself fall back into the darkness, let it fill her until she was one with it. This wasn't the same as when Gaius had taken over her body, or even when he'd guided her to survive the Cradle the first time; no, this was an entirely new, not unpleasant feeling. A trickle, then a stream, then an opened floodgate of power washed through her body. It was as if she'd *absorbed* some of the Cradle itself so that it recognized her as its own. It seemed to flow in and out of her body as easily as air.

Her mind drifted to Winnie, the little girl who had nearly died just yesterday. When she'd been healing her, Ros felt as if she wasn't just using the elemental magic to heal, but as if she had become the magic itself. Now, that same feeling flooded through her, but instead of healing magic, she felt the Night.

"Can you heal her?" Cassian asked.

Ros heard his voice, the deep timbre vibrating all around her. His words tickled against her feet. Feet! She had those, she remembered, and she could feel them now if she wanted to.

"I don't know," Teague said, his softer tone sending a chill down Rosalinde's spine. "It's unlike anything I've seen before. I can dose her with healing, but she goes right back to this state. I think whatever did this is still in her."

At his words, her body seemed to respond, and Ros felt pinpricks all over her skin. For a moment she thought she'd let her whole body sit still too long until she was all pins and needles, but then her mind tipped sideways and the memory of the thorns on her skin fell out. She knew then what Teague meant.

She called out to the Night Cradle as it hummed through her bones. She showed it the memory of Winnie and how her body had been healed, followed by the memory of the black vine and its dark red thorns as they entered her skin. The magic responded to her request. Ros felt that same floodgate-opened power surge through her, pushing from inside her skin until the thorns ejected from her and appeared all over her body.

"That's impossible," someone said.

Ros wasn't sure who had spoken. They were all one now. Ros and the voices and the magic and the air and—

No! she thought. The word was sudden and forceful and undoubtedly her. She wanted to share herself with the magic, to let the power be part of her, but she wouldn't let it consume her so fully that she stopped being herself. That was what happened to Gaius. He had tried to take the magic, and it devoured him.

You can be part of me, but you cannot take all of me.

The ground beneath her grew cold for a fraction of a second before warmth flooded through her entire body. She could *feel* the world around her again as an internal tingling and an external vibration extended through her limbs and her body returned to normal.

Well, mostly normal. Now she had the Night Cradle moving within her, and a deep voice seemed to whisper inside her mind that "normal" would never be an option for her again.

When the strange quavering of her body ceased, and the voice refused to speak again, Ros pushed herself up to a sitting position. She smiled at the men hovering around her, but none moved to check on her. As she surveyed their faces, she found a mix of fear, astonishment, and in Cassian's case, something akin to horror.

"I'm fine," she said, rubbing her hands down still-tingling arms to scrape away the thorns that lingered on her skin.

"This shouldn't be possible," Teague said. He was the first to recover from the shock of seeing her sit up, his expression returning to his normal curious one, and he moved to rest his hand on her shoulder so that he could check her condition with his gift. "You were in a state I've never seen before and, honestly, I had no clue how to help you."

"It was the thorns," Ros said. She pointed to one still stuck to the back of her hand.

Teague reached for it, but Beckett slapped his hand away. "That's Wraith's Grasp. The poison could still be active. Just because it isn't hurting her anymore doesn't mean it can't still hurt you if it breaks the skin."

"I've never heard of Wraith's Grasp," Ros said.

Teague added, "Nor I."

"I'm not surprised," Beckett said, his mouth a grim line. "It's a nasty thing, banned in Talabrih and the surrounding kingdoms for the last few centuries. The scholars have tried to wipe it from history to avoid giving any evildoers ideas, but older Botanical families, like mine, are still familiar with it because of the stories passed down. I've never seen it up close before, especially not in this condition. I've seen a shriveled vine on a shopkeeper's shelf, but never a live piece."

"You say 'live' as if it's sentient," Teague said, somewhat cautiously.

Beckett nodded. "It is. Or at least, it *was* while it was attached to the host. Wraith's Grasp is a parasitic plant that can put you in a comatose state and live off your body until you've withered to dust."

"And now that it's out of her?"

"It should die, I think. Like I said, I don't know a lot about it. Even the old families are just passing down legends and tall tales. The only thing that remains consistent in every story is what it looks like. We're all trained to recognize it, because of how deadly it is."

Ros looked from the crimson thorn to the Night mage still standing at a distance. There was something in his gaze that frightened her. "What's wrong?"

Cassian drew a shuddering breath and asked, "What have you done?"

"I don't know what you—"

"The hell you don't, Rosalinde. This place hummed with power until the moment you regained control of your body."

Beckett said, "I didn't feel—"

"You wouldn't," Cassian cut in. "Only someone with Night house blood would have noticed. But it was there, and now it isn't. Ros knows what I'm talking about."

The men looked at her, and she gave a sheepish grin. She mumbled, "I let it in."

She knew how it must sound to him, after all that had happened with his brother, but this was not the same thing. She could feel the vast power of the Cradle surging through her, but she was still in control. Though she wasn't sure what the magic wanted with her, she knew it was content as it was and it would not harm her.

"I don't know what to say to you right now," Cassian whispered.

"It's not the same thing as what happened with

Gaius. I am not trying to control the power, but neither is it trying to take control of me. It's just here," she said, tapping her chest, "with me."

Cassian ran a hand over the dark stubble on his head, but it was Beckett whose voice cut in, saying, "I'm sorry, but what am I missing?"

Ros stood and pointed to the charred circle around them. Though now that she looked at it, there were sprouts of grass coming through the once black earth. She was certain they hadn't been there only moments before. She sighed and said, "This is the Cradle for Night magic."

"*Was* the Cradle," Cassian muttered.

She rolled her eyes. "This *was* the Cradle for Night magic until I absorbed it. Now it's becoming part of the forest again, I think."

"Right, okay, that explains nothing," Beckett said. "What's a Cradle?"

Cassian said, "They're centers of great power. They're also almost complete mysteries. We have no idea what Ros may have just disrupted by taking that power into herself. For all we know, she may have just eliminated Night mages altogether."

The sudden realization hit her hard. She hadn't considered what might happen to the Night house if she absorbed the Cradle. Ros had only known that it would save her, and somehow, that it was *right*. She worried at her lip for a second, then asked, "Can you still use your magic?"

He stepped through the shadows from one part of the circle to the other side. "Yes, but that's not the point."

The relief set in that she hadn't just stolen his power. So what was he so angry about?

"What is the point?" she asked. "I've been in the dark about everything that's been going on. You've all had secret plans and missions and risks, while I've wrestled with what color dress to wear to dinner. But as soon as I do something for myself, something unexpected that doesn't fit into your plans, something that *saves* me outside of your doing, it's automatically a mistake. Well, guess what: I don't want to just be a frivolous girl attending fancy parties and having more food and money and privilege than I deserve. If I'm going to get the crown back, I want to earn it."

"Do you think we've enjoyed plotting a coup? This isn't some private event you weren't invited to. Everything we've done has been to protect you. Some of us," he said, waving to Teague and Beckett, "got dragged into this against our will. Others of us knew what we were getting into and signed up freely because we believe in you. But all of us, *all of us*, want to know that we're doing this for the right person. So if you want to earn your throne, do it by making things better for *all* your people, not just the ones with the biggest houses and the prettiest words. You earn your crown by being the queen your people deserve."

"How can I be expected to manage a kingdom when

the people who claim to care for me don't even trust me to manage a few secrets?"

"It's safer like this. We keep secrets to protect you."

"I don't need you to protect me," she screamed. A murder of crows erupted from the nearby trees as Ros added, "I need you to respect me and know that I can handle things when I need to."

Cassian's jaw was clamped so tight she thought he might break his teeth. Finally, he growled, "Yes, My Queen."

"Will you tell me what happens next?"

A pause, then he said, "No, My Queen."

She was dimly aware of Teague and Beckett moving away from them, giving them room for what needed to be said. Though grateful for their discretion, her mind could only focus on the man in front of her.

"You can't call me your queen and refuse to answer me. That's not how it works. If I'm your queen, you will tell me what's going on. All of it."

Cassian pressed his palms against the back of his eyes. "Don't you get it? This isn't about trying to keep things from you, and for some of us, it isn't even entirely about trying to keep you safe. It's so much more. But it's all a mess, Ros." He looked up at her, his dark eyes achingly sad. "I can't help you. I don't know what happens next. I can barely keep my head above water. None of this was supposed to happen."

"How can you not know what happens next? Aren't you part of the Rising Tide?"

"They never trusted me enough to tell me anything. I was always just a filthy Night mage to them who could flit around and help them do the dirty work. But it wouldn't matter if I did know. I'm utterly helpless where you're concerned. Don't you understand that yet? I've been lost since the day I met you. Everything I thought I knew flew out the window when you became a real person and not some distant ideal of what a ruler should be...of what a *woman* should be."

"What are you saying?" she asked, breathless, as her lungs seemed to constrict to nothing in her chest.

He closed the gap between them in two quick strides. "I'm saying that I am desperately in love with you and I'm trying to separate who I want to be *with* you and who I need to be *for* you."

She inhaled sharply, taking in his words. Despite all she'd done, the hurt she'd caused him, he *loved* her.

A smile spread across her face, fading only a little when the rest of what he'd said finally registered. She asked, "Can't you be both? With me and for me: be my everything, Cas."

He raked a hand over his head. "I've wanted you to say that, I've wanted you to feel that, but no, no, I can't. Not while I watch you fall in love with another man," he said.

"Cassian, you're mistaken. There's no one else."

"There has only been one thing I've been certain about these last few weeks while I helped plan and plot behind the scenes: I *knew* we would be together. I felt it in my very bones. I was made for you." His voice staggered out of him when he said, "But that certainty was the dream of a fool. It died the day you chose someone else to be your husband."

"You heard Larkin," Ros said. "She forced my hand."

"I heard her, but there's no way to know when she's lying and when she's telling the truth. I don't know if she's working against you or for you, so why would I believe her about this?"

Ros said, "It's true, though. I told my mother I was going to choose you. Florian knew as well. But the morning of the ceremony, I found a note in my room saying that I had to choose Earth house for my father to live. I couldn't risk his life for…"

"For me," Cassian finished.

"For love," she corrected. "It was never supposed to be a love match. That was never in the cards for me. The best I could hope for was to tolerate my future husband. But then I met you."

When Cassian's eyes met hers, Ros felt as if her whole body were on fire. He whispered, "I want to believe you."

"Then do," she said, taking his hand.

Cassian's eyes moved from her eyes to her lips and Ros felt a hunger well up inside her. She wanted to kiss him, wanted to pull him close and never let him go, but as much as she wanted that, she wouldn't force him to be hers, especially when he seemed to feel an obligation to her as the queen. This had to be his choice.

"I want to," he repeated, "but even if the part about

Zandor is true, even if your heart does not belong to him, I still saw you kissing Alaric."

"That was his doing. We'd been separated, and he was just happy to see me. I pulled away."

Cassian nodded. "You did, but that wasn't a one-sided kiss. There's something there between you, whether or not you want to admit it. I saw it that night I snuck into your room when you tried to say goodbye to him to protect his heart. You weren't supposed to love him, but you did anyway. Part of you still does."

"It's history," Ros said. "We've been dancing around each other for a long time, but we've never been on the same page. I always knew we'd fall apart in the end; Alaric, well, he thought we could figure it out."

"Maybe you can."

"No. He's a good man, but we're from different worlds."

"So are we," he said. "But worlds collide all the time. Change is coming, Ros. Hell, you *are* the change. If you want it to be okay for nobles and magicless to marry, then make it that way. It'll take a while for some of the houses to fall in line, but the lower nobility has been doing it for decades under the nose of the law. You can finally make it okay for them, and you can be with Alaric."

"I don't want to be with Alaric," she said. "I want to be with you. You are meant to be my king."

His eyes were full of sadness when he said, "I've longed to hear those words, and I will live on the memory of them until I die, but I can't be the king."

"Why not?" she asked, a tear clinging to her lashes.

"Because Talabrih needs a king who is good, a king who forgives, a king who can unite the Elementalists and the magicless. Talabrih needs a man like Alaric. That will never be me. When I get my hands on my brother, I can be neither of those things."

"We can bring him to justice together."

He shook his head. "I can feel the darkness at the core of me, urging me to do terrible things. Sooner or later, it will win, and I don't know if I'll be able to come back from that."

"I believe in you," she said. Desperation dripped from her words. She was losing him again, and she knew it, but she didn't know how to cling to him when he was pushing her away. "You can find your way out of the darkness."

He traced a finger down her cheek and whispered, "I'm grateful that you believe such things about a lost cause such as me. Your compassion will lead Talabrih into a new era."

"With you at my side," she whispered.

Cassian shook his head. "Harden your heart to me, Ros, while you still can. When I become the same thing my brother is, I expect you to be the one to end me. Until then, do me the courtesy of doing the one thing I cannot."

"And what is that?"

"Stay away from me."

"Cassian—"

He pressed a finger to her lips, stopping whatever protest was forming on her tongue. "I love you, Rosalinde, and I will do everything in my power to put you back on the throne where you belong. I will serve you as long as I have breath. But I cannot be around you. Whether you love me and I'm forced to deny that love, or whether you don't and I'm forced to live in that version of heartbreak... They both hurt with equality. They both leave me torn and withered at your feet. But I cannot stay away, so I need you to do it for both of us."

When she nodded nearly imperceptibly against the finger still pressed to her lips, he stepped through the shadows and disappeared, leaving any words she could give to fall like ash in her mouth.

Fifteen

With Cassian gone and too many questions to answer at that moment, Ros excused herself from Teague and Beckett and walked farther into the woods. Once she was out of earshot and could let herself fall apart without witnesses, she permitted herself a full ten minutes of gut-wrenching sorrow and self-pity. It wasn't pretty. She felt weak and raw and utterly spent, her heart in tatters, her body still recovering, and her mind reeling from all that had just happened.

At the end of the time she'd allotted herself, Ros stood up from the muddy ground where she'd been slumped onto her knees, brushed off as much of the mess as she could, wiped her eyes on her sleeve, and walked back to where the Cradle had been. She might be broken, her throne stolen, and the people she loved scattered to the winds in various states of destruction, but as far as she was concerned, those were not good enough excuses for her to fall apart.

The guys were sitting at the edge of the circle. Though the space had been blackened and devoid of life before, the grass that had grown since she absorbed the power from the Cradle was now bright green. Beckett's head rested against Teague's leg as he sprawled across the ground, enjoying the dappled sunlight filtering down through the trees. Ros watched as Teague lovingly brushed his fingers through Beckett's hair, his eyes unable or unwilling to leave his lover's face. It was such a tender gesture, and for the second time that day, she felt as if she were witnessing something she shouldn't be.

Beckett glanced over at Ros as she entered the once black circle. He gave her a smile that told her he pitied her for whatever had happened between her and Cassian. They didn't have to know the details to understand things hadn't gone well—he was *gone*, after all—but his expression turned softer, passing into something sweeter as he pointed at the nearby ground and said, "Look at the flowers."

They were tiny things pushing their way up through the dead ground, barely visible through the bright grass. She'd been so caught up in her feelings that she hadn't noticed them, but now that she did, she realized they were everywhere. The petals were red—not as bright as a rose or as dark as a black pearl—but somewhere in between. She reached to touch one, but pulled back for fear of another incident like the Wraith's Grasp had caused.

"They're safe," Beckett said, though his eyes were closed, and she wasn't sure how he'd known she'd hesitated. "I've seen them before. They're rare, but not new."

Ros reached down and traced her finger along a flower's velvety petal. "I've watched my mother create majestic arrangements my whole life, but I don't know that I've ever seen anything as lovely as these."

"They are gorgeous, aren't they?" he said, blinking against the sunlight. "The stems are so delicate, they often can't support the weight of the bloom, which is probably why you've never seen them. Most Botanical mages take years to perfect them, if they do at all."

She'd always thought her mother could do anything. Learning there were still things she couldn't do didn't diminish her gifts in Rosalinde's eyes, but somehow made the things she could do seem all the more spectacular. Ros whispered, "That's amazing."

"It is," Beckett agreed. He turned his head toward Ros and said, "Which makes me wonder how you were able to create them with no skill, no thought, and allegedly, no Earth magic."

Ros met his gaze as heat crept into her cheeks. After learning to access more than just her Water gifts in this very Cradle the day she'd fought Gaius, Ros had been keeping her newfound abilities a secret, hoping she could master them before telling anyone else about them. She'd been hesitant to use them, afraid of getting caught, but now it seemed that she was. Hiding her new power seemed to no longer be an option.

She could lie, say it must be a fluke after absorbing the magic of the Cradle, but trying to use the Night Cradle as the reason she was accessing Earth magic was reaching at best, and a bald-faced lie at worst. Alternatively, she could trust Teague and Beckett with her secret. They had trusted her with theirs and fought on her side when things went sideways.

She sighed, steeling herself to say the words she must, while understanding the unlikeliness of it all. "The day before I named Lyzandor to be my husband, I discovered that I have access to more than one gift."

"Impossible," Teague said.

"You've been saying that a lot today, babe," Beckett interjected. "Maybe just start assuming everything is possible, since your list of impossibilities is growing shorter by the minute."

Ros smiled. Part of her had feared telling anyone about the other magic. Not because they wouldn't believe her, but because they *would*. She could barely access the other elements, so saying she had multiple gifts felt strange.

"So you can use Water and Earth?" Beckett asked. "Those are your parents' gifts, so it doesn't seem that weird."

Teague's eyes went wide. "It's a little weird. How many mages have you heard of who could do that?"

"Brogan de Fai, Araminta Delos Santos, Georguina

Delos Santos, Cavalon the Wise..." Beckett counted on his fingers.

"Folktales!" Teague said. "Those are just stories to feed the imaginations of children while telling them about the first magical families in recorded history."

Beckett took the hand he'd used to count and directed his four outstretched fingers toward Rosalinde. "Stories come from somewhere, my love. Our queen here is proof that it can happen."

"As wild as some of those old tales are, I have trouble believing they could hold any truth."

"Don't worry, I have enough faith for both of us," Beckett said. He looked back at Ros and said, "Show me a trick."

Ros smiled down at him, grateful for a person in her life that didn't seem to have an agenda. Beckett truly seemed as if he only wanted the best for Ros, and was willing to accept what was going on with her simply because she'd said it. No pretense, no distrust, no need for reasons or excuses.

She knew he'd expect an Earth gift after what they'd just talked about, so instead she held out her hands and let the bloom of a shadow pass between them. When she'd practiced that in her bedroom, she'd had to lie down afterward. Now it was easy to do, since she had the power from the Cradle.

"Oh, okay, that's amazing, and also a little spooky. Wasn't expecting darkness like that, but you absorbed all the Night magic that was here, so I guess it makes sense. As long as you don't catch on fire—"

Ros snapped her fingers and a flame burst into her hand.

Teague laughed. It was the first time Ros had ever heard him laugh so fully and though it surprised her, she could see it was more to do with Beckett than anything else. At his side, Teague came alive.

After the surprise faded from Beckett's face, he said, "Well then, let's see the next one. Are you going to fly through the air or something?"

She shook her head. Manipulating Air was still a struggle for her. She closed her eyes and let her mind conjure images of summer breezes and tree branches swaying. A second later, Ros felt the wind pick up her hair and swirl it about. When she opened her eyes, both men were sitting up and staring at her.

"It's not much..." she began.

"It's incredible. No one has had these abilities since the first families, if those stories were even real," Teague said, casting a glance at his ever-believing boyfriend. "Why haven't you shown the kingdom that you can do this?"

Ros shrugged. "I thought people would be afraid of me."

Beckett stood and put his hand on Rosalinde's shoulder. "You're the true Queen of Talabrih. The elements themselves answer to your whim. If anything, you'd have the people pledging to follow you through this world and the next."

Teague stood up and took Beckett's hand, saying, "Just like we will, Queen Rosalinde. We'll go where you need us. Through this world and the next."

SHE WOULDN'T MAKE them go quite that far. After sharing with her the little information they had about the Rising Tide and their plans to return Ros to the throne, she concluded their best course of action would be to regroup with anyone who might still be in the city surrounding Earth house. She detested the idea of going back there, especially considering the dark queen could be waiting for her, but there was no other option. Besides, she needed to see if any of her friends made it out of the fire.

Cassian could have told her about survivors, if he was there. Things had been so chaotic before he vanished that she hadn't thought to ask him. Now she was full of guilt for ignoring such a pressing matter, especially considering she'd taken the time to talk about her *feelings* for Cassian when she should have been getting information.

Ros had even thought about waiting for Cassian in case he returned, or leaving a message behind at least, but the thought didn't last long. His words had been the closing of a door and she wasn't sure how or if she should reopen it. Every time there was an opening for the two of them, it seemed to slam shut before either could wedge their foot in to stop it. Perhaps, she thought, that was for the best.

She'd always thought hard work was part of making a relationship real, that working for it made it better, but maybe there was a point where no amount of struggle could repair what was fundamentally broken. As loath as she was to admit it, they'd been building a brittle house on shaky ground. There had always been a kernel of mistrust between them, a shadow of uncertainty that coated every interaction with doubt. Their foundation was cracked, and at that moment, it felt like no amount of work could fix it.

Instead, she would work toward a goal she could reach with help from people she trusted. Even if it was a bit frightening, Ros was ready to take her next steps into an uncertain future.

She stood in the middle of what had been the Night Cradle, a bead of sweat forming at her temple, her hands linked with Teague and Beckett.

"You're sure about this?" Teague asked for the sixth time.

"Yes," she said, her confidence increasing each time she had to reassure him.

"But you've never done it before?" he asked.

"I considered it once, but it was too advanced for me at the time and I wasn't sure exactly what I was doing."

"When was that?" Beckett asked.

"This morning," Ros replied. She didn't miss the

look that passed between them, but she chose to ignore it. Instead she said, "My understanding of Night magic has completely changed since I absorbed the Cradle's power. Not only do I know how to use it, but I understand how it works and how to extend its power to you temporarily."

"It's not that we doubt you..." Teague said.

Beckett laughed nervously, high and pitchy as he said, "Yes, we do. But we're trying not to. That's probably the best you're going to get right now."

"That's good enough," she said. With a squeeze of each of their hands, she said, "Hold on to me."

Ros stepped through the shadows.

Sixteen

⤜⤛⟡⤐⤏

Shadow-walking was different with Ros in control than it had been with Cassian leading her. With Cassian, it was a multitude of flashing lights and bright colors all around them, and Ros could never discern a path. There had been an unbelievable beauty with him forming the passage, like a hundred sunrises combined with fifty blooming flowers drenched in a dozen seas while they flew through clouds made of stardust and wishes. It was surreal, dreamlike, and altogether otherworldly, giving Ros the distinct impression that her own world was just a shadowy copy of something far realer and also far more phantasmagorical than she could imagine.

As she led Teague and Beckett through the shadows without the benefit of a true Night mage to guide them, it was more like a narrow hallway between where she had been and where she wanted to go. The colors were still there, but muted, as if she was looking at them through a frosted pane of glass. Ros noticed more shadows now than when she had walked through this in-between place before. Every time she took a step, spools of darkness spread out from her feet, leaving shadowed footprints in her wake.

The three of them stepped out from the eerie, shadowed hallway and into a large bedroom. The walls were painted a deep shade of forest green, and all around the room were accents in silver. High ceilings with intricately carved crown molding in pristine white kept the room from feeling heavy despite the dark walls, as well as a massive window that took up an entire wall, its light undaunted by the sheer mint-green curtains.

"It's exactly how I remember it," Ros muttered as she turned to take in the room.

"No reason to alter perfection."

She turned to the voice, her breath catching in her throat as she saw Larkin leaning against the doorframe. Ros swallowed against the swell of relief threatening to come out in a sob. "I thought you were..." she started, then shook her head to fight off the emotion threatening to overcome her. She swallowed hard and said, "I'm glad you're not dead."

"Me, too. And I'm glad you made it. I wasn't sure..." Larkin trailed off.

The women looked at one another for a moment,

then both broke into grins. Ros said, "I'm still angry with you."

"You should be."

"I don't know how to trust you anymore."

"I'll earn it."

"And if things don't go back to the way they were?"

Larkin shrugged. "They shouldn't.

"Right," Ros said.

"Right."

There was a long pause while the two stared at one another before Florian popped his head around the corner and asked, "Do you two need the room, or can we get on with this?"

Rosalinde's heart felt light as a feather when she saw him. "You're okay."

"Of course," he said, walking into the room. He gave Teague and Beckett a nod and said, "Glad you boys made it."

Beckett stepped forward and shook Florian's hand. "Same. We heard there was a fire and weren't sure..."

He trailed off, but Florian's brow curled in confusion. "We all made it out. Cassian didn't tell you? Wait, where is he?"

Ros sighed. "Long story. Basically, we didn't get a lot of talk time before he vanished. He's fine, I guess, but I don't expect him to be back with us anytime soon."

"Sounds right," Florian says. "The bastard saves our lives, runs off to be your hero immediately after, then doesn't return so we can give him a proper thanks. What a jackass."

Though Florian tried to keep his tone light, Ros could hear the concern underneath. He knew there was more to the story than what Ros had said, and though he didn't press her for more information, it was clear from the look he shot her that he was worried about both her and Cassian.

Ros forced a smile and said, "It doesn't matter right now. There's plenty for us to do without worrying about what he's doing. We can figure things out with Cassian once we've settled the rest of this mess."

"How do you propose we do that?" Alaric asked.

He was in the hallway outside the room, brawny arms folded across his chest. There was a hardness to his face when he looked at her and Ros felt a piece of her heart break when she met his hazel eyes. Those eyes had always looked at her fondly, even when he was hurt, but now what she saw in them chilled her to the bone: nothing. Alaric looked at her and saw *nothing*.

Though it wasn't the same blackness she'd seen in others when the darkness took them, the emptiness there was nearly as frightening. Ros swallowed and tore her eyes from his. She could handle a lot of things, but seeing how completely he had closed himself off to her was not one of them.

She still didn't believe Cassian was right about her future with Alaric and what it would mean for Talabrih. No matter how much Cas seemed to be trying to push them together, Ros knew their paths divulged for the best. That didn't mean she wanted to absolve herself of their past. Even if their lives were going different ways, she still cared about Alaric and wanted him to be part of her life. Just not in the way he wanted to be.

After a moment, she gathered her composure and did her best to answer the question she'd nearly forgotten that he'd asked. "Nothing has changed. We go with the original plan. Gather the Rising Tide."

ROS WANDERED the halls of the Zolto mansion with an ease she didn't feel in her own home. Larkin's brother and parents were still at Water house and Larkin had sent all the servants home with pay for the next few days. There were only three servants who stayed; they were the ones who lived on the grounds and all had been at the Zolto house for longer than Larkin had been alive. She vouched for their loyalty, and although Ros was still uncertain about how much her word meant, it was the best she could hope for right now.

The lack of people in the house gave it a quiet, deserted feeling. Ros found that she very much liked the solitude of it. It was unfortunate she couldn't stay and enjoy it.

Ros had snuck away under the pretense of finding some sleep in the hours before the rest of the Rising Tide arrived. In truth, Ros was looking for her father. She checked the blood on her palm as she walked away from where the others had gathered, making sure it still pointed in the same direction. Larkin hadn't brought King Tancred to the Zolto house, but had taken him to the nearby Earth house. So, that's where she went.

She had been to Earth house a handful of times in her youth, though not recently. Royal requirements kept her centered around Water house, and since Larkin came to see her often, there hadn't been a need to return. As a kid, she'd often wandered off to find her friends when her family visited the noble house, much to the chagrin of her parents. When she got older and they forbade her from leaving Earth house in search of trouble, she'd lost interest in the trips to the other houses, leaving the diplomatic missions for Elsa instead. Ros wondered if her sister had used any of the visits to make noble connections or if they'd all been used to set up her network of spies.

Earth house was situated on a massive hill with the main street through town leading to its front door. Ros had always been impressed with the intricate door and the delicate gold flowers displayed upon it. When she was a child, her mother told her how the door was created when a Botanical mage married a Metallurgist. He created beautiful blooms for his wife, while she wielded metal to make his creations live forever. They added layer upon layer until at last they had formed the massive door, and here they built Earth house around it.

As much as Ros had always loved the story, she was

glad she didn't have to see the door this evening. Instead, she called on a memory from her last visit and fed it to the power from the Cradle. Ros stepped into a shadow in Larkin's house and out into a maid's closet in Earth house. She couldn't remember the name of the boy who had whisked her into that closet for a few eager teen moments, but she wished she could thank him now.

Ros peeked out of the closet and looked down the hall. A group of servants congregated at the end of the corridor, but the rest of the area was empty. Ros grabbed a bucket and mop from the closet and moved out into the hallway. She still wore the old dress and cloak Clarissa had given her, and her time in the woods had certainly left her looking less than royal. She wasn't sure where her father was being held, but maids were needed every-where, so she thought she could get in most places without a problem.

Larkin had said the king was being held in a guest room, so Ros headed to the upper floors, knowing Earth house had a similar layout to Water house. There should have been guards around the door, giving away his loca-tion, but the hall was empty. She looked at the blood in her hand, hoping she could follow it, but after she inspected the room in the direction it had pointed, she found the blood now pointed west, away from Earth house.

It didn't matter. She would check the other rooms, no matter what the blood said. Perhaps this close to him, it had stopped working.

She was entering another room, mop in hand, when she heard a voice call, "You there, maid. Come here for a moment."

Ros walked toward the voice immediately, head bowed, not stopping until the speaker's shoes were in Rosalinde's line of sight. Ros thought of the younger maids at Water house when they were still timid and unsure, asking, "How may I serve?"

"There's wine all over the bedchamber. Clean it up."

"As it pleases you," Ros said.

She went into the room as directed and began cleaning the wine stains. She had expected a spill on the floor or perhaps a table, but it had not been an exaggeration when they had said *all over* the bedchamber. Everywhere she looked, there were dark red stains.

"Ah, Queen Sariyah, welcome back," Ros heard the woman say from the hallway. "I have a maid attending to your room right now if you'd like to find rest in one of our lounge rooms for a few moments."

Ros cursed at her foolishness. If the dark queen caught her here, *alive,* that would be the end of their rebellion. The Rising Tide might try to power on, but without a queen to put on the throne, their work would all be for naught. She could run, or try to, but if she did, they would know there was an imposter maid and she wouldn't have a chance to find her father.

You're a mage, a voice sang in her head. *Act like it.*

Ros startled at the sound of it. It wasn't her own voice chiding her, but the one she'd heard when she had consumed the magic of the Cradle that had let her know it was okay that things wouldn't be normal for her anymore. It had been soft and had made her feel at peace then. Now though, it was heavy, flowing through her mind like sap, sticking to everything. This voice was distinctly masculine and its words registered as more of a growled command than a recommendation.

But she didn't have time to dwell on this fresh development and the voice was right. She couldn't sit around waiting for something to happen, or run away every time things were out of her control. She needed to own who she was and what she could do, right now and as the future queen of Talabrih.

Ros reached out to the particles of the wine. Though they were quickly drying on every surface of the room, they had once been liquid and she could work with that. She pulled the wine toward her bucket, drawing more and more until the room was nearly spotless.

There was one area of the floor that seemed particularly hard to draw out. Ros stepped toward it and tried to reach out to the wine, but couldn't seem to grab it. With a jolt, she realized the problem: she was calling to wine, but this stain was blood.

She swallowed the bile rising in her throat and tried not to think about whose blood was on the dark queen's floor. Instead, she pulled the blood into her bucket just as the bedroom door swung fully open. Head down, Ros moved to the edge of the room while Sariyah inspected her work.

"That was quite a bit of wine to remove so quickly," Sariyah said, her voice tinged with suspicion. "And so thoroughly."

"We have a wonderful, dedicated staff," the woman who had called Ros in said.

"So it seems."

The woman leaned to Ros and whispered, "Your task is finished. You are dismissed."

Ros gave her curtsy and moved for the door, head low and eyes downcast, even as her lungs squeezed and begged for air. The wrong breath could give her away, and so she held it. She kept her pace steady despite the need pulsing through her to run from Sariyah's chamber as fast as she could. Once in the hallway, she released the breath she'd been holding and inhaled raggedly. She stopped trying to blend in with the rest of the servants and ditched the mop and bucket in a closet.

There were only two rooms left to check, so she raced to the first door. Her father wasn't there. With one door left, Rosalinde's heart hammered against her ribs. He *had* to be there.

Her trembling hand reached for the doorknob to the last guest bedroom. She turned it. The door swung open and she stepped inside. There was an empty chair by the open window and it rocked slightly in the breeze. On the floor beside the chair lay a slim, poorly made gold band. She recognized it immediately as the one she'd made for her father when she'd taken a sudden interest in crafting at the age of eleven.

She picked it up, noting that it was still warm.

Ros placed the ring on her palm and looked out the window, staring in the new direction the drop of blood pointed. Wherever King Tancred was now, he was still alive, but he was no longer in Earth house.

Seventeen

Ros paced in front of Larkin, running icy fingers along the tops of her arms. The homespun clothes were doing little to fight the chill that had come over her since she left Earth house. She couldn't shake it.

Finally, when she could get the words to form on her lips, she asked, "Did you know?"

"Know what?" Larkin asked.

"I swear to everything and anyone listening, if you knew about this…"

Larkin stepped in front of Rosalinde's ceaseless stride, halting her movement. For a moment, Ros seemed to have forgotten Larkin was in the room, as if she'd been talking to her and *not* to her at the same time. Larkin put her hands on Rosalinde's shoulders and said, "Stop. Take a breath. Tell me what's happened."

Ros narrowed her eyes and spat, "As if you don't know."

"How could I?" Larkin asked. "You've been cryptic since the moment you randomly appeared in my bedroom while I was half-dressed. I would have been far more upset if you hadn't seen me mostly naked before. Remember the incident last summer?"

Ros remembered the incident in question, but she wouldn't be distracted with Larkin's foolish antics right now. There was too much at stake. "I went to see my father."

Larkin's face seemed to brighten at this. "And? Were you able to find out anything that can help us?"

"He wasn't there."

"I'm sure that's not right," Larkin said. "The Lady Ruler gave me every assurance that the king would be well-guarded and cared for while in her custody."

"Do you trust everyone at their word?"

"Well, no, of course not. But I trust Valeria. She's not only my house ruler but also a dear friend of my family. There's no reason not to believe she has the kingdom's best interests at heart."

"Does it change your opinion of her knowing that she voted to have me dethroned? That her mother and mine were close friends, enough to sway your house ruler to vote me out? My mother is a guest in her home as we speak."

Larkin's brow creased as she chewed on her lip.

Finally, she said, "No, that doesn't change my opinion of her."

"No?" Ros yelled. "Have you already forgotten that Sariyah tried to kill us?"

"Valeria probably has no idea what caused the fire in town today. Even if she knew, there's nothing she could do but bow to Sariyah's whims. If the Queen Mother comes to visit, you can't turn her away, whether you're a friend or foe."

"And which are you, Larkin? She told her guards not to hurt you because you were one of hers."

"She was lying, trying to confuse you to put a rift between us again. Your mother knows how to get under your skin, but you can't let her push us apart again with one frivolous comment."

Ros was shaking. Larkin might be making sense, if she weren't so wound up, but her father's absence and the blood on the floor of the dark queen's room had left her tense and looking for a fight. She and Larkin were on rocky ground already, uneasy allies at best, so it was easy for Ros to take her anger out on the Earth house noble. Too easy, which was probably why she should stop.

Ros sighed, scrubbing a hand over her face. "There was blood in her bedroom, Lark."

"Why were you in her bedroom?"

"That doesn't matter."

"The hell it doesn't," Larkin said. "I can almost overlook that you went looking for your father, despite the fact that it put all of us in jeopardy. But going into her bedroom was asking for trouble. Do you know what would have happened if she'd caught you?"

"Of course I know! She tried to *murder* me today. And you, too. But it's not like I was looking for her, trying to jump back into the fire. I got stuck in a situation and I dealt with it the only way I could. Don't judge when you don't know what happened at Earth house."

"Yeah, because you won't tell me."

"It. Doesn't. Matter."

"And what does matter to you, Ros? Your friends don't. The future of Talabrih doesn't. The people who deserve more than the terrible hands they've been dealt? Well, you couldn't care less. The only thing in your head is saving your father."

"What's so wrong with wanting my father to be okay?"

"I want your father to be okay because he's *your* father, but I want him to stay gone because he's a terrible king. His disappearance was the first good thing that's happened during his time on the throne."

Ros scoffed, unable to hold back her shock at Larkin's words. King Tancred was a kind, good person. He was a loving father, a doting husband, a good king. He *was* a good king. Wasn't he? She shook her head, trying to dislodge the question and the doubt it brought. Ros said, "Finding him could make all the difference for us. His absence started this whole thing."

"You're missing the big picture, the thing that changes *everything*."

"Explain it then."

Larkin sighed. "Your father's disappearance didn't start this. Nor his father before him. And bringing him back will not fix it, no matter how hard you wish it would. A revolution has been brewing in Talabrih for a long time. Whether it was your father's, or yours, or your child's reign, eventually something was bound to give. All it needed was a catalyst."

"His disappearance was the catalyst."

"No, love, you were. People started hearing rumors about you, about how you care for the magicless as much as the Elementalists, about how you were kinder and fairer than those before you. They started preparing for the day when you could take the throne. Well, that day came, but your chance to change the kingdom was ripped from your grasp by overreaching nobles who wanted the status quo. Only the people will not stand for it this time. The Rising Tide will not be stopped."

Ros couldn't believe her ears. Larkin talked as if the entire country was poised to strike against the monarchy. Sure, the system needed to be changed in some respects, and she would be the one to make those changes when the throne was truly hers and she wasn't just a place-holder until her father's return. That didn't mean the whole thing needed to be thrown out or burned to the ground.

Ros felt her anger fizzling out, but she stoked it for one last accusation: "You were the only one in contact with the Lady Ruler who knew I was in the city. As far as my mother knows, we're all dead. So tell me why my father disappeared as soon as I made it back to Earth house?"

Larkin's eyes narrowed. "After everything that's happened, do you still believe I'm out to hurt you? I'm the one who told you where he was."

"I already knew he was here," she said, holding up her bloody palm. "You saw how close I was to finding him and let me believe you were on my side to distract me long enough to have him moved."

Larkin put her fingers to the bridge of her nose. "You're out of your mind. You see dastardly villains in the people you know and trust."

"The people I know and the people I trust aren't mutually exclusive."

"I'm sorry for what this has done to you. This whole situation with your father, the plots against you in Water house, your mother's betrayal... my betrayal. So much has happened in such a short time that you barely seem like the same person I've known all these years," Larkin said. Her voice sounded so desperately sad, Ros almost believed her.

Almost. These last few weeks had shown her that trust was overrated until there was proof it was deserved. If Larkin couldn't prove her innocence...

Ros grabbed Larkin by the elbow and called to the Night magic coursing through her. She stepped into the shadowed hallway, the muted colors swirling at the edges of her sight while her mind focused on where she wanted to take her sometimes-friend. A moment later, Ros and Larkin stepped out of the shadows, the two of them appearing in a dungeon cell in Water house.

"That's a handy trick, ain't it?"

Ros looked over her shoulder at the man who had spoken. He had been accused of stealing from the royal granary, according to the complaints leveled against him at the last hearing she attended. The man had claimed his village was suffering from hunger and, though he'd petitioned for food with the Elementalists in the town through the proper channels, they'd dismissed him and left his family to starve. Ros had wanted to investigate the matter, but the counselors had convinced her there was no truth to his claims and he was simply a thief. Now she knew better.

"What are you doing?" Larkin said, pulling from Rosalinde's grasp.

"Putting you here for safekeeping."

"You're joking."

Ros shook her head. "I don't know what to believe anymore, Larkin."

"This is foolish. You need my help."

"Maybe. Maybe not. I don't imagine you'd be much help if I'm constantly doubting your loyalty. At least if you're here, I'll know whatever bad things happen have nothing to do with you."

She stepped between shadows before Larkin could say anything else. Ros moved into the cell where the thief was and the man jumped back away from her. She asked,

"Were you telling the truth about why you stole from the granary?"

"Y-yes, Your Highness."

She nodded and reached for him. "Take my hand."

His hand crept toward hers, fear clear on his face, but he took her hand anyway. Ros shadow-stepped from the dungeon to the edge of the town outside of Water house.

"Go home," Ros said. "Tell your people to be ready. Change is on the horizon, but it's going to be messy."

"But you... You'll help us?"

Ros gave a quick nod and said, "Watch for the Rising Tide."

Eighteen

Twenty-eight people. That's how many showed up after she'd told Alaric and the others to gather the Rising Tide. It wasn't an army, certainly not enough to do any damage against the dark queen's forces if it came to a fight, but it was more than Ros had expected to show up considering her waning royal power and lack of prospects for gaining it back.

They were gathered in the Zolto home, though none of the family was present any longer. If Larkin's absence was noticed, no one mentioned it to her.

There were faces she recognized: high nobles Lucretia and Gillium Davenport, Markese Mathews, an older Fire Elementalist of wide-renown, and Florian's cousin, Dryden; most of the other faces she knew were lower nobles whose names she'd never had to memorize, a fact that chastised her now that they were here to support her while she'd never bothered to learn about them.

Most of the people in the Rising Tide were new to her. There were farmers and bakers, blacksmiths, artisans, merchants, and servants. The majority of them were dressed in the colors of Earth or Water, but she spotted a couple Fire and even an Air house worker among them, despite the distance from here to their homes. These were the people who worked to make her and keep her a queen. Their hopes rested on her as the ruler of Talabrih, because they believed she could make things better. In truth, she had no idea why they put so much faith in her.

As she surveyed the room, she realized how much Cassian had been right about. He had gently accused her of not knowing her people, and she had balked at the thought. He had challenged her to speak with those who weren't noble, who had no magic, who had no hope.

But Ros had foolishly believed that because she'd had a few encounters with those people, namely Alaric, that she understood them. In reality, she'd been clueless about who they were and what they needed. It took losing her throne for her to understand why it was important that she keep it. She didn't want the throne for her own power or glory. She wanted to help her people—*all* of her people, especially those that had too long been wronged by the crown and nobles.

She felt a presence at her side and turned to see Alaric. Finding out that Ros had planned to marry Cassian had been a blow, hurting him in a way she never wanted to, but he was still here. He didn't touch her, didn't look at her, but he remained by her side, solid as a rock in a storm.

"I suppose I should talk to them," Ros said.

Alaric's fingertips grazed her elbow, a touch so faint she wasn't sure it was really there. "You can still change your mind. You can leave it all behind and never look back."

"With you?" she asked, unsure what she wanted to hear.

"With whoever you want. Or alone, if it suits you. This is your moment to decide what you want."

Ros didn't have to think about it. She'd watched the faces she knew and the faces she didn't as they milled about, waiting for everyone to arrive. There was hope there, sure, and determination, but there were far too many who wore a mantle of burdens that left them beaten down.

"I want to serve my people. I can't live just for me when I know I can do more. Part of me wishes I could run away from this and experience a life without the burden of my birthright, but I would be cheating myself and the person I was with, because I would never lose that gut-wrenching feeling that comes with inaction," she said. As she spoke her next words, she knew she was saying a true goodbye to him. There was no coming back from this, for either of them. "I loved you, Alaric. I never told you because I was afraid. Our story was always going to end. No matter how much of me wishes things were different, they aren't."

There was a long pause before Alaric said, "I know. I was a fool to think you'd choose me, in the end."

"I didn't choose Cassian over you. Or Zandor. Or anyone else. At least, not intentionally," she said.

"Maybe not," Alaric said. "But even if there was no one else, you'd still always choose Talabrih over me. This kingdom is your one true love."

"I'm sorry," she whispered.

"Don't be. The people need someone who can put their own desires on hold to pursue what's best for the kingdom. It's just my bad luck to be in love with the person who's willing to do that."

Ros took a deep breath and let it out slowly. After all his attempts to get her to run away from her life and her responsibility, Alaric seemed to finally understand who she was and why she could never leave. He understood her just in time to say goodbye.

She said, "I will always care about you."

"And I, you, but I won't keep holding onto hope that you'll change your mind. I'll do whatever I can to get you back on the throne. After that, you're going to need a new blacksmith."

"You're leaving?" she asked, fear bleeding into her voice.

Alaric had been such a big part of her life, she wasn't sure she wanted him to be gone, even if she didn't want him for her own. The selfishness of that contradiction wasn't lost on her, and she felt guilty for it even as she hoped to figure out a way to change his mind.

"I don't know what will happen, Ros. I just know I can't be around you. It's the only chance for me to move on."

She wanted to refute his claim and promise they could figure out a way to remain civil, if not friendly, as long as he would just stay. But Ros knew better than to make foolish assurances where an ex-lover was concerned. As much as she might want him to stick around, Alaric was making the best decision for himself, and she couldn't fault him for that.

Ros gave a nod, not trusting herself to speak. She might understand Alaric's motivation and even agree with his decision, but that didn't mean she wouldn't try to convince him otherwise if given the chance. So, she wouldn't give herself the chance.

Instead, she took a deep breath and stepped away from him toward the front of the room. It was time to address the Rising Tide. It was time to go to war.

ALL EYES TURNED to her as she stepped into the center of the room. She'd been in this dining hall many times before. Unlike those times of lavish dinners and gilded decorations, the table and chairs had all been pushed to the walls to make room for the assembly.

Ros looked among them, letting her eyes meet each of theirs. She wanted them to know how much this meant to her that they would be here. She needed them to know they were important.

There were five people who had slipped in while she was talking to Alaric, and all were surprising to her. The first two were Aggy and her wife. The old woman stood between Beckett and Teague with her arms around each of their waists. On Beckett's other side, a thin woman with silver curls held his hand in hers. Aggy's wife, then, who had shunned her betrothed to be with the woman she loved.

The third surprise was an Elementalist she hadn't seen since the morning she had announced her engagement to Lyzandor Zolto: Graeme Monsanato of Air house. He stood in the back with Florian, something she never would've expected considering how openly hostile they'd been to one another while on the road, but revolutions can do strange things to people, she guessed.

The fourth and fifth unexpected guests were Alaric's brother, Saul, and his wife, Clarie. After all that had happened in the short time she was at their home, she hadn't expected to see them again. But there they were, standing against the wall, trying not to catch anyone's attention. Saul's wore a stern expression, stark in comparison the smile that lit Clarie's face. Ros surprised herself when she realized she was happy they were there.

Ros cleared her throat, a habit she'd taken from her father, as he always did the same before addressing a group. She didn't need to gather their attention, though;

the room was so still, she could have heard an ant crossing a carpet.

"It's a pleasure to see your faces tonight, even under such dire circumstances. Your allegiance is a boon I'll not soon forget. I assume you all know why you're here—"

"To save your royal arse."

Ros smiled. "Thank you, Aggy. You are a wordsmith if ever there was one." There was a smattering of chuckles and Ros said, "You're not wrong. My royal arse does need saving, but frankly, so do all of yours. And the rest of Talabrih's. Our movement may not be large right now, but our goal is massive. Some who are with us are unable to come into the light at this point without risking their positions. We are stronger because they are hidden. More will join us once they feel safe to do so. Together, we can create a kingdom that's better for all of us."

She saw some heads nodding, but unsurprisingly, the nobles were not among them. Ros motioned to the Davenports and said, "You have some concerns."

Mr. Davenport had the grace to look sheepish, but Mrs. Davenport lifted her chin and said, "I want a better kingdom, Your Highness, but I don't want to lose what I have."

"You have more than half the town put together," a voice spoke up from the side of the room. Ros didn't know the man, but his clothes marked him as a laborer.

"I worked hard to get where I am. I earned it, and I won't support a cause that tries to take it from me."

"I didn't realize being born into a magical family was

such hard work," the laborer said. "Must be why the rest of the starving townsfolk haven't done it—we don't want to work for it."

"Now, now," Ros said. "This isn't why we're here. We need to come together despite our differences, not grow more divided."

"So that you can grow into the same leader your father was?" another person asked.

"I am not my father," Ros said. "I want to create an equal kingdom where people can grow into prosperity, but that doesn't mean I aim to take what you have."

"You're saying you don't mind that she can slaughter a cow every night of the week while the rest of us are fighting for scraps?" the laborer asked.

Ros bit her lip. This was not going how she'd planned. She thought these people were already on her side, not that she needed to win them over. Then again, maybe they were on her side, but they were not on one another's.

"There are a lot of things that need to be changed to make things better. Food supplies need to be reviewed by an impartial distributor to prevent the issues you're talking about. We shouldn't have one family dining in extravagance while children's empty stomachs rumble down the street. Same with shelter. Everyone deserves a home. We need a better distribution of wealth. Access to medics. There's an intense, uneven power dynamic between mages and magicless that shouldn't exist. Mages should *help*, however they can, whenever they can. These are just a few things I've noticed recently and I want to address, but I know there are so many more and I promise to listen so we can figure things out together. But I can't do anything about them from a spare room in Earth house; I need help returning to the throne."

At least one thing she'd named seemed to have struck home with those in the room. She opened her mouth to drive it home, when the door to the dining hall burst open and Kalin, the dark queen's guard, came panting into the room, blood dripping from his side.

"She's coming," he stammered, then fell to the floor.

Teague pushed through the crowd and dropped to his knees beside the man. He pressed his hands against the wound and poured healing into him, but after a moment, he pulled his hands back and stared at Kalin's blood upon them. It wasn't enough.

A clang of metal drew her attention away from the dead body on the floor. From the sound of it, the Zolto's front door had just been forced from its hinges.

She looked at the people in the room as panic sank in. "Fight if you must. Run if you can. This isn't a battle we're prepared to win, and I don't want you dying for a lost cause."

Ros strode to the entrance where Kalin lay and forced the doors fully open. The dark queen was coming and though Ros might not feel ready, she could give her mother hell on the way to her grave.

Nineteen

The Zolto family had been smugglers before they went legitimate a couple generations back. Larkin had mentioned it on numerous occasions, because unlike her parents, who were mortified by the idea of impropriety, Larkin reveled in it. So, as soon as the dark queen's forces arrived, Ros instructed the others to look for the tunnels. Of course, Aggy hadn't needed the directive—she was pulling away the hidden panel while Ros was yelling the order.

Alaric had given Ros one last long look, then he'd grabbed the sword at his belt and charged through the secret tunnels to secure safety for those who would follow. Ros was glad that nearly everyone *did* follow. She'd been afraid there would be far more heroes among them than the fierce-hearted rabble that stood here now. This group, though, made her heart swell with pride. They may be small in number, but they were fierce.

Florian, Graeme, Romenia, Beckett, Teague, and Brisa had fanned out behind Ros, ready for battle. As much as the sight of them buoyed her, Ros had shaken her head and said, "Beckett, I need you to get Romenia out of here."

"I'm not going anywhere, My Queen. I belong at your side."

"You've already been hurt protecting me," Ros said, nodding to her broken arm and bruised face. "And for some reason, you're refusing to be healed."

"Stubborn," Florian muttered.

Ros ignored him, adding, "I won't let you die for me."

"You'll have to remove me bodily," the guard said, planting her feet.

"Then that's what we'll do," Ros said.

Beckett's vines had bound her legs together without her noticing while she and Ros had been arguing. With a nod from Ros, he tightened them and they tripped her. Graeme's air phoenix caught her before she hit the ground.

"Can you help them?" Ros asked the Air mage.

"Of course," Graeme said.

"Teague, you as well. You're more useful out there than you are down here."

His brows knit together. "I could reverse my healing, theoretically, and cause death instead of life."

"No," Ros said, without even the slightest hesitation.

"There's enough death already. I'd rather you stay on the side of good. Obey your morals."

Relief was clear on Teague's face as he nodded a farewell to her. She'd known he didn't want to hurt anyone—he spent his life devoted to healing—and it had been difficult for him to offer to do it. Maybe she should have considered it, but doing so would make her as bad as the others vying for the throne. She couldn't do the same things they would.

As the four of them headed for the tunnels, Florian said, "And then there were three."

Ros shook her head. "You need to take Brisa as far from this fight as you can."

"What?" they both asked in unison.

"She's the last of the Delos Santos line. It's her secret to keep, and I'm sorry to be sharing it without permission, but someone else needed to know, just in case. She may be the only person who can truly unite both the nobles and the magicless. She needs to be protected at all costs."

Florian looked at Brisa, eyes wide. "Seriously? Why the hell didn't you say something? I would have definitely curbed my language in your presence. Probably."

"I don't want the throne," Brisa said, her mouth a flat line. "But I want to make sure someone worthy gets it. That's why I'm here."

"If I die today, you'll need to step up. You can't keep hiding in the shadows of Night house while Talabrih burns. Can you do that?"

Brisa swallowed, nodding. "Whether or not I want to do it, I'll make sure Talabrih has a queen who will take care of *all* her people. By the elements, I really hope it's you and not me."

Boots echoed down the hall, marching toward them. Ros said, "Go, now. I'll hold them off."

And she did.

She blasted the forces with wave after wave of water so cold her fingers ached to send out the magic. Still, they kept coming.

Ros shot another blast of freezing water down the hall. The guards struggling toward her were washed back, but more took their place as they fell. She'd pushed back half a dozen advancing groups and there didn't seem to be an end to the dark queen's forces. She didn't see them, their faces hidden behind her blasts of water, and that made it somewhat easier to keep fighting them. The idea that some of them could be her former friends and acquaintances ate at her resolve.

She pressed on.

After so long she'd lost count of how many waves of soldiers she'd driven back, Ros had to admit the awful, undeniable truth: she was getting tired. She was a strong Elementalist, but she'd never trained to fight this many people at once. At best, she'd dueled three mages and a handful of swordsmen in a training session, but it was different facing down row after row of bodies that kept materializing in front of her while she tried not to kill anyone.

They'd chosen their profession when there wasn't a war, and Ros knew some of them would leave if they could, so she did her best to give them a chance to walk away. If they could still stand after her barrage of water, maybe those who wanted to leave would have enough sense to escape in the chaos.

Ros hadn't seen her mother yet. She wasn't surprised. It was a textbook tactic to use the magicless as fodder to break down an opponent's defenses. Such little imagination. Unfortunately for the dark queen, it would not work.

When enough time had passed that Ros was sure her friends had made it to safety, she stopped hurling waves down the hallway, stepped into the center of the room, and waited for the guards to come. When they reached the entrance to the dining hall, Ros said, "I've given you plenty of chances to turn away, but this is your last one. I don't want to kill you, but I will if I have to."

One of the guards stepped forward and said, "We're here to protect Talabrih from a traitorous queen."

"If that's the case, why are you still serving her? It's my mother who is a traitor against the crown."

"You'll not speak ill of the Queen Mother, traitor scum."

"We know what you did to the king," another yelled. "His blood is on your hands."

Ros flinched at the words. Though she knew she hadn't harmed her father, it still pained her that these men and women could think her monster enough to kill him. She shook her head and said, "You've been misled. Though I could have killed you instead of drenching you and saved myself both time and strength, I let you live because I care for my people. I will not let the dark queen's lies be the reason for your deaths."

And with that, she stepped through the shadows and out into the garden.

SHE SHOULD HAVE KNOWN her mother would be waiting for her there. Even with the darkness in control, the garden was her mother's sanctuary. It had seemed too pedestrian for her, but perhaps the darkness truly was out of ideas and choosing the simplest things to get by.

Night pooled around them, thick with anticipation. The dark queen's lips twisted in a hideous smile. "When I heard dissenters were gathering, I should have known you'd be among them."

"The people won't stand for what you're doing," Ros said. "They'll fight to keep their kingdom from falling into the darkness."

"Then I'll kill them all."

The dark queen surged forward, knocking Ros to the ground. The two rolled over field and flower, crushing everything in their path. Thorns tugged at their clothes, ripping the fabric and scratching every inch of bare skin.

They rolled into the trunk of a tree. Her mother landed on top. She pressed her hands to Rosalinde's throat. Thick rope-like plants wrapped around Ros, twisting her limbs nearly to the point of breaking, and pulling her down into the ground.

Ros called to the Fire element. It answered her easily, like always, though she had no real familial ties to it. Fire responded to her needs almost as easily as water, springing to her fingers and igniting the plants that held her. Several melted away, others slithered off her, but all seemed to issue a tinny wail that filled the air in the surrounding garden.

More vines sprang up, pulling against her harder than before and trying to drag her into the ground. Ros tried to call to Fire again, but the vines encircling her neck grew tighter and she was seeing black at the edge of her vision. She couldn't call the magic, even the ones that came so easily. She couldn't even think.

Ros felt the dark queen banging her against the ground and screaming, "Why won't you just die?"

The vines pulled her out of her mother's grasp, down into the earth that had just opened up below her. Ros felt dark soil pour over her face. It trickled into her nose and mouth and she choked on it. The more she coughed, the more fell into her mouth.

She heard the dark queen reciting a children's song about ashes to ashes, dust to dust, in a terrible singsong voice.

Ros knew she was going to die.

"Must I do *everything*?" a silky voice asked.

It was the same voice she had heard before when

she'd been in Earth house, though she didn't know where it was coming from. Maybe she was losing her mind. It didn't matter now, since she would be dead soon.

Ros felt a jolt of power. Her body was moving, but not under her control. A moment later, she was back in the garden, on her knees, coughing up dirt. The voice said, "You're welcome," then returned to silence.

The dark queen turned from dancing on her daughter's grave, caught sight of her not-dead prey, and said, "Are you *kidding* me?".

Ros fought to catch her breath before the next attack began. But there wasn't a next attack. Ros cleared the dirt from her face, and through eyes bleary with tears from coughing, she saw the dark queen locked in a battle of magic with...

"Cassian?"

"Get her out of here," he called.

Ros stood and took a step toward him, readying herself to fight. As she called on her magic, an arm swung around her waist and pulled her into the air. *Graeme.*

"Put me down!"

Graeme's grasp grew tighter instead. She watched Cassian and the dark queen growing smaller in her vision as she and Graeme rose up, up into the sky. She tried to call on the Night Cradle so she could step through the shadows to help Cassian, so she could free herself from Graeme and face the thing that had taken over her mother, but the magic wouldn't answer.

Over and over she called out to it, in her mind and

against the buffeting wind, but the power was silent, and she couldn't think of any reason it should be. The voice had saved her only moments before—why had it gone silent again when she most needed it? Even the spark of Night magic she'd been practicing with prior to absorbing the Cradle wouldn't respond to her.

Out of harm's way yet again, the weight of all that had happened crashed down on her all at once and her body went limp. She had narrowly survived being buried alive, but she was still breathing. From the looks of it, her friends had made it out, too. Though at least one of them had been foolish enough to return for her.

She wanted to thank Graeme almost as much as she wanted to smack him. Leaving Cassian again in the throes of battle with the darkness was the worst thing she could possibly think of. He'd forced her away once in an effort to protect her, and now he'd done it a second time. The worst part was that both times she'd *allowed* it. She'd permitted herself to be rescued when things got tough, when she wasn't sure she could handle it, when she almost didn't. That wasn't the action of a queen, but a coward. What she was still refusing to admit to herself was that some scared little part of her even wanted it.

Twenty

Ros wrapped her arms around Graeme's waist, her fingers digging into the skin of his stomach. Several times she tried to look behind her for any sign of what had happened to the others, but there was nothing to distinguish their battleground from any other piece of land from this high up. The air buffeted her as if it wanted to rip her from the phoenix, but she tucked her head down against Graeme's back and held firm. It was taking too much of her strength to simply hold on, and in the end she was forced to stop looking for her friends—for Cassian—and focus on making sure she didn't fall.

"Where are we going?" she yelled. Her words were snatched away as soon as they left her lips, and for a long moment she thought Graeme hadn't heard her.

He suddenly banked west and said, "Home."

She wasn't sure what to say to that. She'd expected

him to take her somewhere out of harm's way, thanks to Cassian's insistence, not to remove her from the fight so completely. Ros thought they would land a few miles away, she would recuperate, and then she'd be able to shadow-walk back to the fight. But she could have never predicted he would take her all the way to Air house.

Maybe she could rest in flight and find her way back when they landed.

As if reading her thoughts, Graeme said, "You can't go back. This is a one-way trip."

"I have to."

"You'll die if you do. You aren't strong enough to go against your mother right now."

"Neither is Cassian. Maybe if we do it together..."

"Cassian is trying to save you. He knows his limits. All he was trying to do was distract her long enough to get you away. Now that he has, he can make sure the others are safe and help them regroup. He'll come for you when he can."

As she watched the land zip by beneath them, traveling faster than she'd ever imagined, she wondered how long it would be before she saw Cassian again. Minutes, hours, days? Graeme made it sound like this was all part of the plan, but did that plan involve seeing her after he told her to stay away? Would she see him again, or was he only there to rescue her and disappear yet again? Even if she did see him again, she had no clue what she would say. The very thought of Cassian made her brain feel muddled. She'd felt so certain about him only a few weeks ago, but now everything had changed.

If she didn't return for him now, if she waited at Air house like Graeme seemed to want, it would take nearly a week to get to Air house by horse, assuming Cassian couldn't just shadow-walk himself there. She wasn't sure if he'd ever been there; she wasn't sure he would even come, despite what Graeme said.

And if he came for her, what did it mean? She knew he cared about her—he'd thrown himself into harm's way to save her—but was it loyalty for his queen, or his love for her? It was impossible to know. When he'd seen Alaric kiss her, it had hurt him, she was sure. She saw the pain on his face; it was the same pain she'd seen the day she was forced to choose Zandor instead of him. Though she'd offered him words and promises and vows of affection, nothing seemed able to bridge the gap. The truth of her feelings meant little to him when it came down to deciding to be with her or get retribution against Gaius. Cassian was a man who always got his revenge.

Even as she thought about it, overcome yet again with her feelings for the Night Elementalist, she wanted to smack herself. She was in the middle of a battle, not just for the throne, but for all of Talabrih. And though she'd been removed from the field, the fight raged on. Yet here she was, consumed by thoughts of Cassian, a man she'd only met a month ago, who'd challenged and saved her, but who also kept pushing her away. Ros had always considered herself an independent woman who didn't need a man to make her happy. To a degree, that was still true. But there was something about that infuriating Night mage that made her certain she would be happiest with him at her side, even if she had to struggle harder than she thought should be necessary to make it happen.

They flew on in silence, Rosalinde's thoughts alternating between her desire to make things right with Cassian, her annoyance at herself for caring as much as she did, and quite a bit of guilt that she couldn't think of anything else.

When Ros saw the blue-tinged mountains and their snowy peaks, she knew their journey was almost over. The Air Elementalists had perched themselves far beyond the reaches of the magicless who lived near the mountains that marked Talabrih's borders, using their magic to keep their spires afloat where none but their own could gain access.

It was a cruel thing in Rosalinde's eyes, the thing she most hated about Air house, and the reason she'd refused to accompany her parents on the rare occasions when they'd visited. It wasn't uncommon for Elementalists to have a high opinion of themselves, but to go so far as to elevate your home so that commoners couldn't reach it? Despicable.

But there was nothing she could do about it now or as the queen. That was their house business. Maybe they would someday have a house ruler with a good head on their shoulders who would despise the lofty spires for what they were. Maybe that ruler would be Graeme.

As the spires materialized in the fog ahead of them, Ros had to admit they were as beautiful as they were awful. Sea lavender and slick with a glittering sheen that somehow seemed to glow in any weather, they looked like the upside-down tears of giants suspended in the sky.

Pressed against Graeme as she was, she noticed when he took a deep breath and let it out slowly. Though he hadn't said a word, Ros knew what he was feeling. There was a profound satisfaction in going home, especially if you'd been away for a while.

But Graeme hadn't been away long, had he? She wasn't positive, but she had thought he'd returned home after the ceremony that crowned her queen. Maybe his home was more important to her than she realized, and the sight more consuming.

They looped around the top of the tallest spire, their circles growing smaller with each pass until their air phoenix came to a gentle stop. Graeme hopped down with ease, then turned and put his hands on Rosalinde's waist, lifting her off his nearly invisible beast.

As her feet touched down on the strange pale stone, her breath was stolen from her, leaving her gasping. Graeme seemed unharmed as he grazed his hand along the neck of his steed, smoothing wild feathers with his delicate touch.

Ros tried to get his attention, half uttering his name as she tried to get a breath. He didn't respond, keeping his back to her as he continued to caress the bird and whisper softly to the creature.

A moment later, the crushing against her chest lessened enough for her to take a full breath. She sucked it in greedily until at last she felt satisfied. She still felt weak, as if someone had snatched away every ounce of energy she possessed, but at least she could breathe.

"Are you finished?" Graeme asked, turning toward her.

Ros looked up into his pale eyes, one dark eyebrow arched high on his forehead. "What's happening to me?"

He folded his arms. "You're fine. It's just a bit of magic poisoning."

Magic poisoning?

"Come on," Graeme said, stepping toward the entrance to the spire. "It's too cold to stand around up here spelling your ruin when I can do it from inside instead."

Ros found her feet locked in place as she watched Graeme start down the stairs. No, she must've misheard him. He had rescued her from sure death. Why would he do that if he was out to get her?

Graeme had been her savior, not the villain in her story. He was supposed to be one of the *good* guys. He glanced back at her once before descending fully from view, and the look on his face told her all she needed to know. There were no good guys, no heroes, to come to her rescue this time. The only way for her to win was to save herself.

Ros forced her body into motion, running toward the spire's edge. She would use her Tsunami magic to catch her. She flung herself at the perimeter...but it flung her back.

She landed hard on the top of the tower as tendrils of air pushed her down. Ros put a hand on the cold stone and forced herself back up. She tried to call on her magic to defend herself from the air, but as soon as she touched that spark inside her where the magic resided, it felt *wrong*. Polluted. She couldn't access it, much less call it forth to be used. The magic poisoning restricted something that had been inside her since birth.

Her fists balled at her sides as anger coursed through her. But anger did no good. Try as she might to stand against the buffeting winds, they slid her inch by inch to the door Graeme had gone through until there was nothing she could do but resign herself to follow.

He was waiting for her at a landing close to the top. Without bothering to look at her, he said, "Took you long enough."

"Oh, I beg your pardon," she cooed. Ros wasn't sure why that was the first thing she went for, with all the rage and frustration boiling inside her, but she was glad she did. The softness of her reply seemed to rankle Graeme more than any yelling could have.

He sneered. "Tried to jump, didn't you?"

She didn't answer, instead turning her head toward what he was looking at. It was a large, round room that filled most of the floor, leaving only the small landing at the stairway where they stood. The room itself wouldn't be significant if it wasn't for the floor-to-ceiling glass window set into the room. It gave a prime view of the room from their vantage point, with nary a place to hide.

Inside the room was Cordelia le Fevre, Florian's missing sister. Rosalinde's memory shot back to the night she stood with Graeme away from the campfire after he and Florian had argued. Graeme had told her about his love for Florian's sister, how she had borne a child and given it away, then disappeared before he could make things right between them.

"Was it all a lie?" Ros asked.

"Not all of it," he said, staring at Cordelia. "I *did* love her."

"You don't know what love is," Cordelia said, her tone brittle and empty. She didn't bother looking up.

Graeme's face distorted in an instant, fury bunching his features close together as his face reddened. "What have I told you about talking back to me?"

"It doesn't matter," Cordelia said. "If I talk, you're angry. If I don't talk, you're angry. There's nothing left in you but anger."

Ros wondered if the darkness had taken control of him like it had before, but no, his eyes were still pale. Whatever had made him this way was of his own doing.

Graeme took a deep breath and turned his face into something less hostile. "Come along, Rosalinde. This girl offers no entertainment. But I believe you'll take a keen interest in the next act."

Her stomach twisted like a pit of vipers. There was

nothing about this perverse game that interested her. "Doubtful."

"Look at the blood on your hand."

Ros flipped her hand over to the drop of her father's blood that had so strangely pooled in her palm and directed her toward him for weeks. It had always pointed to Earth house, but he'd been removed only minutes before she got to him. Now, the blood didn't point in any direction. It was still.

Her eyes flicked from the blood on her palm back to where Graeme had been, but he was already descending the stairs below her. She almost called out to him—almost. She wouldn't give him the satisfaction of that, but she had no choice but to follow him down the steps in search of her father.

ROSALINDE'S her heart hammered against her ribs. Just before she was out of earshot, she heard Cordelia say, "Be careful, My Queen. Even polished monsters have claws."

She descended to the next landing. Graeme leaned against the wall, his face a mask of boredom. Ros was certain he was thrilled with himself on the inside, but he didn't show her that. It was as if he wanted her to think this was all easy for him, that torturing others and toppling kingdoms was just a menial task on his list of things to do.

Ros turned to the window, stepping forward until

her face nearly touched the glass. The room wasn't lavish and furnished like Cordelia's had been. Hers had seemed like one of the palace guest rooms transported into a prison. A symbol of Graeme's love, perhaps. Not this place. It was dark and dank, the sour stench of mildew permeating the whole floor.

She didn't see him at first. The shadowed room served to make him invisible. But as her eyes adjusted, she saw the dark shape huddled on the floor, unmoving.

"What have you done to him?" she whispered.

Graeme stepped forward until he was beside her. He held a small silver key in one hand and an unlit lamp in the other. "See for yourself."

She didn't know where he'd gotten the lamp—he certainly wasn't holding it a few minutes ago—but she didn't really care. The only thing that mattered was getting to her father. After these last several weeks trying to figure out what happened to him, where he was, and if he was alive, it was all she could do to take the key and lamp without breaking down into a sobbing mess. There wasn't time for that. Her father was *right there*, and he needed her.

Ros lit the lamp and moved past Graeme to the door at the side of her father's cage. "Door" was a much fancier name than it deserved. The entrance was so small, Ros had to crouch low and suck in her breath as she crammed herself inside. But she made it, and that's what mattered.

She ran to him, falling on her knees to wrap her arms

around him. She bounced against an invisible barrier, her arms thudding against whatever stopped her a mere inch from touching him. Ros pushed her fists against the blockage. She felt around, looking for a way through, but there was a wall of air keeping her away.

"Father," she called, her voice echoing through the chamber.

He looked up, but the face was one she barely recognized. Larkin had said he was a guest at Earth house, but from the look of him, that was far from the truth. His skin was ashen and hanging loose on him. There were dark bags under his eyes. He wore a shabby mustache and beard that covered his mouth, but still she heard his tattered voice mutter, "Rosalinde?"

"It's me, Daddy. I'm here."

She heard a click behind her as Graeme closed and locked the door. *Stupid, stupid girl,* she thought. Now she was just as trapped as her father had been for this last month.

"That was far easier than I expected. Uncle Hessian thought you'd put up more of a fight."

"Hessian," she hissed. She'd known he had a hand in this since the second she learned her father was missing. Still, from the way they had argued in the hall, the way Graeme had stormed away and sided with her, she hadn't realized they were in cahoots.

"He knew you suspected him, but none of us were sure how deep that suspicion ran."

"Clearly not deep enough."

"This whole thing could've gone entirely different, if only you'd had the sense to choose me."

"If that's what you wanted, why tell me to choose Earth house?"

"We didn't," Graeme said, brows furrowed.

"So the note in my room," she asked, "wasn't part of your plan."

"That conniving little..." he muttered.

And just like that, Ros realized the biggest mistake she'd made thus far. When she saw the note from Larkin, she'd seen it for a threat, telling her to choose Earth house or her father would die. But it had never been a threat. Larkin was trying to keep her father alive by throwing off the Air house's plans. She'd been telling the truth, or at least as much of it as she knew. Her best friend had been trying to *save* the throne, not take it.

"What part did Earth house play?" Ros asked.

Graeme sneered at her. "You are such a fool. And, it seems, so am I."

He turned to walk away, but Ros called out, doing the thing she most hated—she begged. "Please, don't do this. Don't leave us here like this."

Graeme glanced over his shoulder. "And how exactly should I leave you, Your Highness? A king presumed dead, a queen dethroned... you're no use to me."

"We can be. Return us home and I'll marry you. I'll make you the new king. Air house can rise in power."

He smirked. "No need for that. Once I bring word to your sister of the battle at Earth house, how I saw you and your friends murdered and how I alone escaped to bring her the message and pledge my forces to defeating her enemy, she will be appreciative enough to take me as her new ally and, eventually, her husband."

"You're betting a lot on a woman you don't know. Elsa is strong and sharp. She'll see right through you."

"Your sister is not the person you think she is, nor will this be my first encounter with her. I've been putting in my time with her at Water house, so our relationship is already established and lends itself to this ruse. Perhaps you've even seen us walking through the gardens?" he asked, quirking a brow. "I have no doubt my plans will work."

"And if they don't?"

"Whether or not it works, by the end of this year, I will have killed your sister and taken her place as ruler of Talabrih. The only thing she gets to decide is how much longer she lives."

He marched down the steps without another word. Ros leaned against the air wall, her body sagging with the weight of all she'd just learned. This was it. Every hope she'd had of making it through this mess was finally gone.

There was a tapping on the air wall and she heard her father say, "You can't let him win, my darling."

Ros turned and looked at her father. At what was left of him, anyway. Though she saw a shell of the man he was, when her eyes met his, the spark that had always shone bright in him remained. He might not look like the father she knew, but he was there in the way that mattered.

"I don't know what else to do," she said.

She wanted him to tell her it was okay, that she tried her hardest and that was all she could do. Instead, he looked her dead in the eyes and said, "That's a bunch of manure."

"Wh-what?"

"I thought I was pretty clear," he said, raising his brows. "Get off your arse, stop feeling sorry for yourself, and let's figure out what we can do."

So she did. Because he was her father and her king. Because he was right. And, mostly, because he'd never sworn at her a day in his life, and she wasn't sure exactly what to do about it.

Ros sat up and faced him, resting her hands against the air wall and wishing with all her heart that she could simply reach over and embrace her father.

"You found my blood," he said, pointing to the mark on her palm.

She nodded. "I'm sorry I didn't do more with it."

"At least you knew I was alive," he said. "Does that mean the Night mage is on our side?"

"Yes, and his mother, too."

Her father's eyes widened at that, but he didn't comment further. Then he pointed at her other hand and said, "Where did you get that one?"

She flipped her hand over and looked at the palm. She'd all but forgotten her bargain with Whimsy. Maybe there was hope for them yet.

"What day is it?" She did the calculations in her head, trying to gauge the phases of the moon during the chaotic days that had just passed. She murmured, "I think I have time. Just barely."

She looked up to give her father a quick smile, but there was fear in his eyes. "Ros, do not move."

"What's wrong?"

"There's something behind you."

"You didn't call for me, Rosalinde Adara Managold," a voice behind her said. "The moon has completed its dance, and you didn't call."

It was a voice she recognized, singing of silver moonlight on dark waters, clear summer nights bathed in pale light, the glow of unrealized potential.

"I was about to," Ros said.

She turned, expecting to see the fae from the forest, but the thing before her was something entirely different. Where the Moonchild had been small and fair, this creature was massive, nearly double Rosalinde's size, and covered in coarse, dark hair. She had marveled at how dainty and lovely Whimsy had been, but this thing was the stuff of nightmares, beastly and terrifying to behold.

"About to, you say," Whimsy's too-sweet voice said from the monster. "But that wasn't the bargain."

"Ros, no. Tell me you didn't make a bargain with this *thing*."

Whimsy growled. "Spoken like an average human. No regard for *things* it doesn't understand."

Ros ventured, "Perhaps he would understand better if he saw you as I did when we met before."

"Ah, but you saw me in the moonlight, child. There is none of that here."

"So without the moonlight, this is what you look like?"

Whimsy nodded. "My dark form is not pleasing to your eyes. It is not meant to be. I am not here to offer sweet words and kind gifts. I am here to take what is mine."

"No, please," Ros begged. "I was going to call you just moments before you arrived. I swear it."

"You had a moon to choose your favor, girl, and you did not. That is not my fault."

"So much has happened," she said.

"Yet you allowed my boon to waste away when you could have had my help at any time."

"I didn't want to use it wrong."

"Your reasons are of no concern to me. A deal has been struck, and I've come for my due. Now tell me, what is most precious to you?"

Ros racked her brain, searching for anything that could help her out of this. But there was nothing. She'd found little in the library about the fae, and what she had found was barely more than fairy tales or nursery warnings.

"I have nothing precious," she began, but Whimsy's

laughter cut her off.

"A lie I've heard a thousand times. I do not need you to choose, Rosalinde Adara Managold. I can read your eyes as easily as a book."

Ros didn't know if Whimsy was using a turn of phrase or if they truly meant it, but either way, she closed her eyes in an attempt to avoid giving anything away. It lasted only a second before there was a sharp intake of breath and Rosalinde's eyes jerked open to see Whimsy on her father's side of the air wall. Whimsy lurched toward where the king remained frozen in fear.

"No, please," she said. "I just got him back."

Whimsy paused at her words and tilted their head. With a nod, they said, "I will not take him from your sight again. Though from his sight, and all who know you, you'll be removed."

They reached forward with a long finger and touched the tip of her father's head. Without another word, Whimsy vanished.

"Father," Ros said, banging against the air wall. "Are you alright?"

Her father looked at her curiously, a puzzled expression creasing his brows. "I am well, Miss. And you?"

"Miss?" she repeated. "Father, it's me, Rosalinde."

King Tancred scratched at his head and said, "I'm sorry, I don't recall having the pleasure of your acquaintance."

Ros felt as if the wind had been knocked from her. After all she'd been through to find him, all the horrors she had seen this past month, and now—elements help her!—now her father didn't recognize her. Whimsy had left her father's body, but taken his mind, or at least his memories of Rosalinde. Whimsy had taken something precious from Ros, and in its place was a stranger wearing her father's face.

She grit her teeth together and muttered, "This is not our end. This is not where our story stops. One way or another, I will get my father back. I swear it on all that is good and right in this world and the next. So I hope you can hear me, Datura Whimsy, because our bargain is only just beginning."

Afterword

Thank you for reading *The Secrets of Earth House*. I hope you enjoyed the continuation of Rosalinde's adventure! If you did, please leave me a review, stop by my website, or find me on social media. I'd love to hear from you. You all mean the world to me and I'm truly thankful for the time you've given my book.

If you'd like to try another story with royals, magic, and new book boyfriends, check out my mermaid series starting with *Black Sea Bright Song*.

You may also like my sci-fi series under Shelly Jarvis: The Book of the Golden One duology starts with *The Dreamwalker* or the 3-book post apocalyptic series Little Star begins with *Even Ghosts Have Teeth*.

About the Author

Michelle Jarvis is a fantasy romance author with a penchant for royalty. She loves diverse characters and believes everyone deserves a love story.

While Michelle has had her own love affair with writing since she was in elementary school, it wasn't until her late thirties that she realized how much fun it was to turn up those romantic subplots. Now she's combining her love of fantasy and her newfound passion for romance to put them into the hands of readers.

Michelle lives in West Virginia with her partner and their rescue dogs–Gimli, Gus-Gus, Pickles, and Fergus–as well as Ethel Furman the bunny who also thinks she's a dog.

For free books, bonus scenes, and news about upcoming releases, sign up for Michelle's mailing list on her website: www.authormichelle.com